thank you, LUCKY STARS

BEVERLY DONOFRIO

schwartz & wade books · new york

Published in the United States by Schwartz & Wade Books, an imprint of Random House Children's Books, a division of Random House, Inc., New York.

Schwartz & Wade Books and colophon are trademarks of Random House, Inc.

Visit us on the Web! www.randomhouse.com/kids

Educators and librarians, for a variety of teaching tools, visit us at www.randomhouse.com/teachers

Library of Congress Cataloging-in-Publication Data

Donofrio, Beverly.
Thank you, Lucky Stars / Beverly Donofrio—1st ed.
p. cm.
Summary: Ally has looked forward to a new school year, especially since she and her best friend, Betsy, have planned since kindergarten to sing in the fifth grade talent show, but Betsy has a new best friend and Ally, shy and prone to cry, is targeted by bullies and a strange new student who is looking for a friend.
ISBN 978-0-375-83964-1 (trade) – ISBN 978-0-375-93964-8 (lib. bdg.)
[1. Best friends—Fiction. 2. Friendship—Fiction. 3. Talent shows—Fiction. 4. Bullies—Fiction.
5. Schools—Fiction.] I. Title.

PZ7.D72225Tha 2008
[Fic]—dc22
2007000853

*

The text of this book is set in Plantin.
Book design by Rachael Cole

Printed in the United States of America

10 9 8 7 6 5 4 3 2 1

First Edition

For Jacki Lyden and Linda Cholefsky

✳ Chapter One ✶

I could hardly believe it was here: the First Day of Fifth Grade. The sun was shining through my window, birds sang a hallelujah chorus, and I could feel a case of the heebie-jeebies coming on. That's when my whole body tickles and I jerk around like I've just heard the funniest joke in the world. I even made up a poem.

> The fifth grade is
> Too great
> To even contemplate.

Thank you, Lucky Stars, my best friend, Betsy, and I would be in the same class—for the first time ever. And the event I'd been looking forward to since kindergarten would finally happen—Betsy Jane O'Malley and me,

Ally Theresa Miller, would star in the Annual Fifth-Grade Talent Show. We were going to sing "Bridge over Troubled Water," and I was counting on getting a standing ovation.

I leapt onto my bed and heebie-jeebied, careful not to bounce too loudly because if my mother caught me she'd act like I'd just set fire to the whole state of New Jersey.

Just then my mom called, "Hurry up, Ally! You don't want to be late," so I jumped down and put on my new pink leggings and butterfly jersey. Betsy had the exact same outfit, and we were wearing them together for the first day. First days are the best. Everything is new. Besides your clothes, there's the new teacher, your books, the classroom and where you sit. Everything begins all over, fresh—nothing is ruined yet.

Before I ran to breakfast, I brushed my hair into a ponytail and fastened it with my new rhinestone clip. The clip was identical to Betsy's, of course. Both Betsy and I have honey-brown hair and blue eyes. My hair is thicker and wavy, kind of like a horse's tail, plus I'm taller and skinnier than Betsy. But we're so alike that I figured as soon as our teacher, Mrs. Joy, saw us, she'd probably say, "Are you two twins?" I had a feeling I'd be Mrs. Joy's pet. I'd collect everyone's homework and be the one chosen to answer the principal's phone during lunch on the days her secretary went home early.

I hoped I'd like Mrs. Joy as much as I'd liked Ms. Brady, my favorite teacher, from the third grade. Ms. Brady moved to the Rocky Mountains of Colorado, where she said deer walk right up to your porch.

We live in New Jersey. There is such a thing as Jersey cows, which I think are supposed to come from here. But if a cow walked up to somebody's porch on my block, Mr. Winters would probably just shoot it like he shoots those poor pigeons for sitting on his drainpipe.

I gobbled down my breakfast, called out, "Bye, guys!" to my parents, and ran all the way to the bus stop.

As soon as I got there, that pest Artie Kaminsky, who has annoyed me since the first grade, called out, "Here comes Ally-oop, the Poop."

When Artie acts like a two-year-old and chases me with worms, I run away. When he calls me dumb names, I ignore him. So instead of shouting, "Shut up, you turd ball!" I pretended I'd just had an operation on my eardrums and couldn't hear a word he'd said. I stared up the hill at Betsy's house, wishing she'd hurry up.

When I saw her walk over in a jeans skirt instead of our outfit, my jaw dropped to the sidewalk. "Why are you wearing that?" I practically yelled. I didn't even say hi.

"Wanted to." She shrugged, then smiled at someone behind me.

I heard "Hey, Bets," and turned to see Mona Montagne, our sworn enemy, wearing the same skirt.

"I can't believe you!" My heart was hammering so hard you could probably have seen it through my shirt. "You promised."

"I didn't *promise*. You're such an exaggerator." Betsy rolled her eyes at Mona, who rolled her eyes back.

Betsy and I had been enemies with Mona since she'd moved onto our road in kindergarten. But this summer, coincidentally, their families had rented beach houses just three doors away from each other. When Betsy got back, I'd called and invited her to walk to Lala's Market with me, and on the way I'd asked her about the beach. "Did you guys hang out?"

Betsy had shrugged. "A little."

"What'd you do?"

"Nothing. Forget about it."

"Are you going to be friends with her now?"

"I told you, forget it."

"So you *like* her?" I stopped in the middle of the sidewalk, but Betsy kept on walking.

"Don't make such a big deal about it," she said.

"So why won't you answer my question?" I caught up to her.

"You never know when to give up. You exaggerate everything."

We'd bought Jolly Ranchers, and on our way home, I tried to stop being mad by telling her about the awesome thunderstorm we'd had while she was gone. Lightning had struck a telephone pole on our road and electrical wires had whipped in the wind like sparklers. The electricity had gone out, and all along the street we could see houses flickering inside, all lit up from candles. At her door, Betsy had said, "Wow, I wish I'd been here," and I thought everything was back to normal.

But now everything was the *opposite* of normal. Betsy was friends with Mona.

I pictured them at the beach, walking to the end of a long jetty, then sitting on a rock above the waves, their families in a circle toasting marshmallows around a bonfire, singing "Michael, Row the Boat Ashore." My family never went on vacations. My parents only liked cruises by themselves. Mona's and Betsy's parents were young. Mine were as old as Obi-Wan Kenobi.

I know you're not supposed to wish bad things on people, but if Mona Montagne had tripped at the bus stop and then fallen off the earth, I would have done an Irish jig.

When she and Betsy started whispering, I lost it. I pretended to sneeze and covered my face with my hands. I would have died if they caught me crying.

"Watch out!" Artie yelled, then yanked off my rhinestone clip.

"Give it back!" I grabbed for it, showing my face.

"Make me, crybaby!" Artie ran in a circle around me. "Crybaby, crybaby, wash away your tears, baby," he sang, and the rest of the kids picked up the tune.

✳ Chapter Two ✳

WELCOME was printed in pink chalk on the blackboard in my new classroom, and Mrs. Joy, my new teacher, was sitting underneath it at her desk as we filed in. I already knew that Mrs. Joy was as old as a grandmother and a lot of kids didn't like her. Still, I decided not to be prejudiced against her. Old people can be nice, like my parents. Plus, I figured with a name like Mrs. Joy, maybe she'd be the happy type and make us do crazy things like the Mexican hat dance.

I'd grown taller during the summer and thought I should sit in the back so I wouldn't block anyone's view. I sat down in the last seat of the middle row and waited for Betsy to come in, praying that Mona was in the other fifth-grade class. Thank you, Lucky Stars, Betsy walked in alone. Still, she didn't look at me and sat as far away as possible—in the front seat next to the windows.

Mrs. Joy took attendance in alphabetical order, asking us to raise our hands when she called our names. When she got to "Ally Miller," she asked, "Is Freddy Miller your brother?"

"No," I answered. Teachers had asked me that since kindergarten.

Most teachers hadn't liked Freddy Miller, and I could tell Mrs. Joy didn't like him either. I'd never even laid eyes on the juvenile delinquent. But he was probably in high school by now, setting fires in trash cans. Any day his name would appear in the police blotter in the *East Meadow Eagle:* "Boy sent to correctional facility for throwing hand grenades."

I could tell Mrs. Joy didn't believe that Freddy isn't my brother, because she said, "I'm putting you up front where I can keep an eye on you."

As I moved, I could feel the whole class watching. I tried not to concentrate on how everyone was thinking, *I'm glad I'm not you.* But the only place my brain would go was to how I'd been a crybaby at the bus stop, I'd have no one to play with after school or on weekends, and now Betsy and I would never sing in the talent show.

Tears flooded my eyes.

"Miss Miller," said Mrs. Joy. "You should know right off the bat, all of you, I will not tolerate dramatics. You can go into the hall until you can control yourself. Or please go see the nurse."

I slunk out of the classroom, slid my back down the wall, and sat on the floor. I tried to stop thinking of things that would make me cry. I imagined how if I kept crying so hard, my tears would stream over the floor, then down the stairs. When it was time to change classes, everyone would slip and slide, crashing into each other and falling. Ambulances would screech up, and then police cars. I'd be arrested and put on trial for hurting so many kids. A picture of me crying would appear on the front page of the newspaper with the caption "Public Menace." Every mother and father in town would think, *Thank you, Lucky Stars, she's not my daughter.* I'd be thrown in jail for the rest of my life, which might not be so bad, because then

I'd never have to come back to Heady Hollow Elementary School.

Snot was drooling from my nose. I wasn't allowed to go to the lavatory without permission, but this was an emergency. I had to blow.

In the bathroom, after I blew my nose with toilet paper, I was able to stop crying. But I could see in the mirror that my eyeballs were red, so I tried to think of something to make me happy and turn them back to white. I imagined that my mother won the lottery and my parents took a cruise around the world. My mother hired a butler and a maid to stay with me, and wherever I wanted to go the butler drove me, and whatever I wanted to eat the maid cooked for me. My parents sent presents all the time, like an elephant from India, which I rode around the yard. The maid let Betsy come to the house whenever she wanted, and the butler took us to the mall. I bought me and Betsy tons of stuff, even makeup, with my mother's credit card.

Staring at myself in the mirror, I remembered how Betsy thought my fantasies were dumb and never wanted me to describe them to her. But my fantasies make me feel better. I could see that my eyes weren't that red anymore, so I blew my nose one more time and headed back to class.

As I slid into my seat directly in front of the Wicked Witch's desk, I didn't look at anybody, and thank you, Lucky Stars, they weren't looking at me either. They were all too busy staring at a strange girl standing in front of the class next to Mrs. Joy's desk. She was wearing pink leggings just like mine, only too short. Mrs. Joy was saying that her name was Tina Tamblin and that she'd just moved to town.

"I moved from Amherst, Massachusetts," the girl announced without anyone's asking.

"Yes," said Mrs. Joy. "And we're not going to hold it against her just because she came from someplace different, are we, people?"

Tina kept talking. "Massachusetts was where they had the Boston Tea Party, which started the Revolutionary War. My mother had to move here for a new job, and she said, 'Well, New Jersey's the Garden State, and I love to garden, so looks like we're in luck.' "

"All right, Tina, you may take your seat now."

"But I'm wondering, what kind of garden is New Jersey famous for, vegetable or flower?"

"Tina, I asked you to return to your seat. I don't know what it was like in your old school, but in my class we only speak when we're spoken to."

"What if I have a question? Can't I raise my hand?"

"Of course."

"Excellent. My grandfather says you learn by asking questions. And learning is what—"

I could hardly believe my eyes—Mrs. Joy stood up and hit her desk with a gavel! "In this classroom, when I tell you to do something, you do not ask why, you do not *talk* about it, you *do* it. Now go." She pointed her long curved nail at the desk behind mine, then opened a book. "Everyone take out your math books and turn to page four."

"Math," Tina said. "My second-favorite subject!"

That girl was either brave or crazy. One thing was for sure—she was the funniest-looking kid I'd ever seen. She was skinny as a praying mantis, with tiny little teeth, pop-out ears, and a very big nose. Below her too-short leggings you could see every inch of her bright yellow socks dotted with ladybugs. Her hair was in pigtails that stuck out like donkey ears. She had the look of someone who still played with Barbies, or had a pet snake.

I promised myself never to wear my leggings again.

✗

At lunch Mona and Betsy sat together whispering, their arms touching.

I sat at the farthest table in the farthest corner.

Sometimes I can trick myself into forgetting where I am and go somewhere else, like exploring under the ocean and finding cool stuff on the *Titanic*. But I hardly had a chance, because all of a sudden there were yellow socks with ladybugs next to my feet.

"Hey!" said Tina. "We're wearing the same pants. Don't you know anybody? Why are you sitting all alone?"

"Because I want to."

"In Amherst I had a best friend. Her name was Kirby. Kirby thought her name was weird. But I like it. Don't you?"

Even a girl like Tina had a best friend. I'd only had one friend my whole life—Betsy. I'd never wanted to play with anyone else. I stared at my piece of pizza.

"What's your name?" Tina asked me.

"Please? Could I please just be alone?"

"I just thought you looked lonely."

I concentrated on my pizza, thinking, *Go away.*

Tina cupped her hands around her mouth and called through them, "Earth to Girl with Ponytail, vessel in retreat." Then she walked backward and sat down at the other end of my table. "Shiver your timbers, over and out."

George Bello was sitting across from her. George brought his violin to school every day and propped it in his lap on the bus like a baby. He got special permission during recess to stay inside and practice. He always wore the same thing: khaki pants, a red shirt, and white socks with black shoes. Since kindergarten.

"Hi, I'm new," I heard Tina say to him.

"Hi." George bit into his pizza as Karl Kraus sat down next to him. Karl had won every spelling bee since the first grade and had a tutor for special math because he was so smart. Once I saw him eat a booger. Karl's only friend was George Bello. George's only friend was Karl Kraus.

"Hi, I'm Tina," Tina said to Karl.

"Hi. I'm Karl with a *K,*" he said, then burped.

"You're excused," Tina told him; then the second I lifted my pizza, she called, "Watch out, it's hot."

* Chapter Three *

"**H**ow many times do I have to tell you, ladies do not slam doors," my mother called from the living room, where she was watching *Oprah*. My mother's pet peeves were slamming doors, jumping on beds, jumping period, burping, farting, and yelling. I'm supposed to act like a "lady" even though I'm still a kid.

"Sorry," I called, walking quietly into my bedroom. I silently pulled the door shut and dropped my books on my desk, then flopped onto my bed. I stared at the spidery cracks in the ceiling, thinking how nice it would've been if Betsy had walked home with me. We would've sat on my bed and told each other every little thing about the first day.

I remembered one Sunday, earlier in the summer,

when we'd come back from Lake Tocahonset with her family. It had been almost midnight when we got home, and Betsy's mother had let me sleep over. I took my shower first, then waited for Betsy, all cozy under her comforter in the air-conditioning. When she wriggled in, her hair smelled like coconuts, and her feet were so cold, I jumped out of bed and heebie-jeebied, which started us on a giggling fit. We fell asleep with our legs touching. But when I woke up, Betsy was on the other side of the bed with her back to me. I'd felt so sad even though I knew she'd just turned away in her sleep.

What had I done to make Betsy suddenly ignore me? We'd always said Mona was a snot and a big pain. Her mother brought her to the beauty parlor to put streaks in her hair to make it blonder. Mona blew it dry, shiny and smooth, like a doll's. Nobody but Mona had five different-colored pairs of shoes.

I wished Betsy would go to Mona's house and it would stink like cabbage, and that her parents would walk around in their underwear. But obviously girls with five different pairs of shoes didn't have parents who walked around in their underwear.

I pulled the phone to my bed.

What if Betsy hung up on me?

I dialed her number, then dropped my forehead to the mattress as the phone rang.

She answered!

I sat up straight. "Hi, it's me. Want to come over?"

"Not really."

"Are you mad at me?"

"Not really."

"Then want to ride bikes or something?"

"I'm doing something else. Sorry."

"You're not really sorry."

"That's the trouble with you, Ally. You can never take a hint." And then she hung up.

Hint? Did that mean I was supposed to just accept that my best friend hated me now?

I hugged my pillow over my face so my mother wouldn't hear me crying.

After dinner I went to my favorite spot in the house—the basement. My father had made a room down there with a sofa, two chairs, and a bar. One time my parents had had a New Year's Eve party in it, but usually no one ever went there except for me.

I jumped up onto the back of the sofa and slid down the pole that held up the ceiling in the middle of the room. I kept doing that until I was bored; then I twirled around the pole till I got dizzy and had to sit on the floor.

When I was in the second grade I took tap and ballet at Ms. Janet's School of Dance. One whole wall was a mirror you could watch yourself in. I didn't like to look. Ms. Janet used to tap her cane—"Ally Theresa, one, two, three. Count, two, three. Rhythm. Rhythm. Breathe." I could do it, sort of, but sometimes the heebie-jeebies took over like a swarm of bees. I'd *relevé,* two, three, but for each count I'd do a little hop. I couldn't help myself. It was like I had jumping beans inside me. Once I tried to run up the wall like in my favorite old-time movie,

Singin' in the Rain, but I fell on my shoulder and had to get a cast. After that my mother said I couldn't go back to dancing lessons.

I got up from the floor and used the pole as a partner to disco dance. But it wasn't much fun, so I put on a CD I got from a yard sale that went, *"Oooh, so hot! When you rock you rock, when you roll you roll, up is down and down is up, cold is hot and hot is cold. Jump and shout and rock it all out."* During the chorus, I sang, *"Honey, you can try. Honey, I don't lie. Honey, you can fly. All you have to do is try."* I heebie-jeebied, fell to my knees, and spun like a record. Then I made my head go in circles while I punched my arms like a boxer. I jumped onto the sofa, I slid down the pole, I twirled like a ballerina, I leapt like a deer. When the song ended, I collapsed on the sofa. Everything was still and calm and quiet except for the beat of my racing heart.

✳ Chapter Four ✳

It was like being in the middle of a bad dream. Mona the Menace was wearing *my* rhinestone clip in *her* ponytail.

I hadn't noticed till we sat on the bus, me two rows behind Mona and Betsy. And then I had to find a distraction to pop my eyes back into their sockets. I fixed on the bald spot at the back of Lenny the bus driver's head.

But the next thing I knew, my eyes were zeroing back in on my rhinestone clip. And they stayed there all the way to school.

As soon as we got off the bus, I tried to rush past Mona and Betsy, but then I smelled Betsy's coconut shampoo and exploded. "That's my clip. Artie Kaminsky stole it from me! Give it back!"

"Oh, boo-hoo." Mona wiped her eye with the back of her fist.

"You know that's my clip," I told Betsy. She'd been with me when we bought it from a circular rack at Hammond's pharmacy. We'd both tried on sunglasses. She'd acted like she was a movie star and I'd acted like I was blind.

"You are out of control." Betsy pushed past and marched through the school doors with Mona marching right behind.

✳

I decided to spy on Betsy and Mona after school. I walked really quietly through two backyards on my block until I reached Betsy's next-door neighbor's. I hid behind a big tree in the middle of their yard, and even though I couldn't see Betsy and Mona, I could hear them. They were singing "Bridge over Troubled Water"—the exact same song Betsy and I had planned to sing in the talent show!

I silently dropped to my hands and knees, then lay on my stomach and belly-crawled to a bush on the border of Betsy's yard. Peeking from under it, I could see them sitting cross-legged on the grass. Their feet were bare and they faced each other. Betsy was playing her guitar and Mona was hitting her knee in rhythm with a long weed. I had to admit Mona sang a lot better than I did. They could even harmonize.

When they finished the song, Mona chewed on the weed and said, "I bet we win."

"It's not a contest," Betsy said. "I wish it were."

Mona flopped onto her back and stared at the sky. Betsy flopped down next to her. "I always see old men with white hair, like Santa or George Washington," Betsy said. She was making out pictures in the sky like we had always done.

"The moon, at night when it's full?" Mona said. "Doesn't it look like the man in it is watching you?"

"When I was little I was scared of him," Betsy said.

"Me too. I used to make my mother shut the shade."

Betsy tick-tocked her feet back and forth. And Mona tick-tocked her feet too.

And then it hit me like a rock: Betsy and Mona weren't together to be enemies of me. They genuinely liked each other. They'd both been afraid of the Man in the Moon when they were little. But I'd thought he was my friend. They were alike, and I was different.

I crawled backward out from under the bush, choking back tears. As soon as I reached the tree I'd hid behind, I stood and ran like the wind, tears streaming down my face. I ran by Sissy, my next-door neighbor, the six-year-old pest, who was pouring sugar down an anthill. I ran across my yard, under the willow, and into my house. The door slammed behind me.

"Ally?" My mother followed me into my room. "What happened?"

I hid my face under the pillow, and the words poured out. "Betsy's best friends with Mona."

"Since when?" My mother sat next to me on the bed.

"The first day of school."

"Oh, honey." She petted my arm. "Girls will be girls. No sense working yourself up about it. First you and Betsy were friends. Now it's Betsy and Mona. Next thing you know it'll be you and Mona. These things happen. It's part of growing up. Now, come on, stop your crying." She lifted the pillow from my face and handed me a tissue.

I blew.

"You want to put on some music and help me in the kitchen?" She stroked the hair out of my face. "Dinner's in an hour. You can whip the cream for the pie."

*

The next day after school, I looked out the picture window in my living room and saw Betsy and Mona with Charlie Mordarski and Gracie Finkle. Charlie was a girl—one of the richest and prettiest in school—whose real name was Charlotte. She took horseback-riding lessons and had a purple streak in her hair. Gracie lived around the block and had a baby sister she sometimes wheeled by my house. She also played the organ and the clarinet. My mother said talent like Gracie's was given before birth.

I watched the four of them link arms and do the Yellow Brick Road skip down the middle of our street. Then one of them said something that made them all laugh so hard they broke apart. Charlie pushed Betsy; then they all ran after Charlie, laughing so hard that Betsy stopped, bent over, and called, "I'm peeing my pants!"

I wanted to step outside to see where they were going. But I'd die if they saw me, so I stayed inside, picturing them piling into Betsy's kitchen and sitting on stools around the center island. Betsy's mother would make them Lipton chicken noodle soup with peanut butter and jelly sandwiches. Betsy would peel off her crust and feed it to her dog, Dixie, under the table. She always did that.

✳ Chapter Five ✳

I was so desperate for another kid to do stuff with that I was even looking forward to my thirteen-year-old cousin Francesca's visit. Which means I must have been insane. When Francesca goes to college, she's going to major in torture. She used to lock me in an old wardrobe in the attic for hours. Her favorite thing to do was sit on my chest until I cried uncle and then not let me up. She even convinced me once that I was adopted.

I hadn't seen Francesca for a year, because she lives in Washington, D.C., and her parents only visit every fall. When she and her parents walked into our kitchen, the first weekend in October, I couldn't believe my eyes. Francesca had breasts, and was wearing a bra. She couldn't wait to drag me into the basement to tell me about it.

Without even asking how I was or anything, Francesca sat on the sofa and patted the cushion. "Wait till you start getting breasts," she whispered, even though there wasn't another person in sight. "They itch worse than poison ivy. But you can't scratch them unless you're, like, alone in your room. Because they're your *breasts*. It's so harsh. Want to see them?"

"No!" I covered my eyes.

"Your loss." She shrugged, then whispered even more quietly. "We have this man gym teacher who told us to cross our arms over our chests when we play volleyball. Like, I thought we were supposed to *hit the ball*? Some girls stuff tissues in their bras to look like they have them. You probably won't get them till high school. No offense, but you're kind of immature. Even my mother says so."

I had a feeling she was telling the truth about her mother's saying that, and wondered what made me immature.

"You *are* tall, though," Francesca continued. "It's

probably a hormone thing. Don't worry. They have drugs for that. Hopefully you'll stop growing before you're as tall as those Amazon women. They really existed, you know."

I'm not *that* tall. But I didn't argue with her because I was too busy wondering if you could still lie on your stomach once you had breasts.

"Boys snap your bra strap in the hall," Francesca said, reaching around her back to demonstrate. It actually made a snapping noise. "They call them headlights, knockers, mangoes, melons . . ."

I could just hear Artie—Barf. Puke.

"Come on," she said, zipping up her sweatshirt. "Let's walk to the green."

The green was where a million middle school kids hung out.

"No way," I said.

"Fine," she said, marching up the stairs. "I'll go by myself."

Francesca knew perfectly well that my mother wouldn't

allow it. Being a good hostess was part of being a "lady." So I zipped up my sweatshirt too and followed her up the stairs.

"Where're you going?" my mother asked on our way through the kitchen.

"A walk," Francesca lied, sort of.

"Dinner's in two hours. Don't be late."

"We won't," I said.

At the green about twenty kids, probably all from Andrew Greeley Middle School, were hanging out in clusters on the ground or sitting in pairs on the fence. As soon as we stepped from the sidewalk onto the grass, Francesca started flipping her hair off her shoulders and puffing her lips out. She probably thought it made her look pretty, but it just made her look like a fish.

We sat on the fence, and the minute two girls walked by, Francesca snagged them. "Hi. Got a smoke?" she asked.

The girls looked at each other, then shrugged. The one wearing a striped knit hat said, "Sure," then dug a pack out of her shoulder bag.

"Marlboro Lights. My fave," Francesca said, reaching for one. She put the cigarette in her mouth, then took the girl's lit cigarette. She pressed the lit end against her cigarette, took a deep drag, and shook her head to whip her hair around. "Francesca," she introduced herself.

Thank you, Lucky Stars, she didn't introduce me so I could keep pretending I was invisible.

"Sophie," the girl with the hat said.

"Alice," the other girl said. She'd been smiling the whole time like she'd just heard a joke.

"I can't wait till high school," Francesca said, and blew a smoke ring. "You get to smoke in Senior Court. It's chill. You're supposed to be a senior, but everybody does it."

"We can't even smoke in the parking lot," Sophie said.

"D.C., where I live, is a *city*. It's way cool. You can take the subway practically anywhere. Not like here. Small towns are like desert islands. No offense. But you have to get your parents to drive you to the bathroom. I mean, East Meadow doesn't even have a mall. I'm serious, you should visit D.C. someday."

"Cool," Sophie said. "Hey, we got to go." She nudged Alice with her shoulder, and they walked off without saying goodbye.

Francesca hopped down off the fence. I was afraid she was going to chase after them, but instead, she headed in the direction of home. "If you tell a soul I smoke," she said, looking straight ahead, "I'll tell your parents you shoplift."

"Francesca!" I almost yelled. "You are such a liar."

"Don't test me," she said, walking faster.

"You're going to get cancer." I kept up.

"It's none of your business what I do with my body."

After a while she said, sort of kindly, "You're shy, little cousin, aren't you?"

I didn't say anything.

"You'll never be popular if you're shy, you know. It's a law of the universe."

I'd never thought about being popular before. But

now I thought how Betsy had friends and I didn't, which made her popular and me a reject. I wondered if being shy was something you could grow out of.

Francesca and I didn't talk the rest of the way home. I was glad, because I was thinking. I was thinking that because Francesca is my cousin, I have no choice; I *have* to hang out with her. Maybe it had been the same for Betsy with Mona at first. Maybe their parents had become great friends at the beach, and Betsy kind of had to be friends with her. What could Betsy do if her mother was always inviting Mona and her family over?

That night after Francesca and her family had left, I thought about calling Betsy up, but it was too late.

✳ Chapter Six ✶

Finally, this notice appeared on the school bulletin boards.

> Fifth Graders:
> Can You Dance, or Sing? Play an
> Instrument? Put on a Skit?
> Come Perform in the Annual Heady
> Hollow Fifth-Grade Talent Show

Overnight, in the halls, in gym, at lunch, the talent show was all anyone talked about. I overheard Gracie Finkle telling another kid in the hall that she and Betsy were forming a band! Betsy would play guitar. Gracie would be on keyboard. Mona would be the lead singer, and Charlie Mordarski would play drums. Charlie could beat boys in races. It made sense that she'd play the drums, because she was an individual.

Even Stu and Artie were going to do something: Tae Kwon Do to music.

In class, I was too busy thinking about the talent show until Mrs. Joy asked me to recite two rhyming lines.

"Honey, you can fly. All you have to do is try," from the song I danced to in the basement, came to mind. Then from out of nowhere, Courtney Fine popped into my head too. In the first grade she'd spun in front of the class on a day when she'd forgotten to wear underwear. To this day, every time I see Courtney Fine I think about that. It just goes to show you how one embarrassing mistake can ruin your whole life.

I froze. My mind went totally blank. I told Mrs. Joy I couldn't think of anything.

She took a deep breath. "Surely you can come up with *something*. Use a nursery rhyme."

It felt safer to stare at my lap.

"I'm not standing up here for my own edification, people. Please, do not waste my time. Ally Miller, when you go home this afternoon, you will write in a perfectly legible hand two rhyming lines, one hundred times."

I heard grunting and turned around to see Tina waving like she was trying to land an airplane.

Mrs. Joy took another deep breath, then closed her eyes. "Yes, Tina."

Tina darted out of her seat to the front of the class. She held her hands behind her back and recited, "When I was very small—"

Mrs. Joy pounded her gavel. "Tina! I'm only going to say this one more time. Never leave your seat in this class unless I tell you to."

"I was trying to recite a poem I wrote—"

"If you have something else to say, please raise your hand and wait to be called on."

As soon as Tina sat back down, she started waving again, making a groaning sound like a rusty fan.

Mrs. Joy ignored her.

A few minutes later, I felt something tap my elbow. It was Tina; she handed me a note:

> If Mrs. Joy would swallow a pencil and die
> What a wonderful world this would be.
> Bye-bye.

I almost giggled. Then I stuck the note in my backpack to throw away.

At lunch I got my hamburger and waited with my tray for Tina to sit across from George and Karl. If I sat down first, she'd sit across from me.

Betsy sat with Mona and their band, all of them laughing and talking, kneeling up on their chairs, sipping from straws.

I decided to be brave and sit with Alicia Wong and Mary Dundee, but they said, "Sorry, taken."

So I sat at the other end of Tina, George, and Karl's table, as usual.

"What are you going to do, Ally?" Tina called over to me, talking about the talent show.

"Nothing." As I said it, I knew it was true. Even if there was something I could do, I'd have to do it alone, which I never would.

"George?"

"Ditto."

George attended violin competitions all over the state and won. If I were him, I'd sign up so fast my body would be a blur. The talent show was the only way to change from being a nerd to being popular in a single night.

"George's ears are so finely tuned," Karl said, "all that bad music would turn his eardrums into bongos."

George blew his straw wrapper at Karl.

"Hey!" Karl balled it up and whipped it back. "I bet your mother will make you. Ms. Creeley will force her." Everyone knew that Ms. Creeley, the principal, was George's godmother.

"Oooh, I have an idea. Let's all do something

together," Tina said. "I got it! We could do an act of illusion. I know how to make smoke onstage."

"Dry ice," Karl said.

"Can you make the smoke green, Mr. Techno Wizard?" Tina asked.

"Anything's possible," Karl said.

From having listened to their conversations every day, I knew that Karl could rig up all kinds of contraptions. When he grew up he wanted to be one of those techno guys like in *Mission Impossible*.

For some reason George wiggled his ears.

"I got it!" Tina jumped out of her chair in a cheerleader jump.

Betsy's table looked over.

"After the green smoke clears, the audience would see us all standing on the stage. Me and Karl could each hold the end of a sheet and make it go like waves. I saw it in *The King and I*. And Ally could hold a cardboard boat at her hips and go all wavy like she's sailing down a river. George could play 'Swanee River' and wiggle his ears. I could touch my tongue to my nose. Can you guys do anything funny?" she asked me and Karl.

I burst out laughing. I couldn't help myself.

I hadn't said one word, but I could tell by the way Tina smiled over at me that now she thought we were friends.

✳ Chapter Seven ✳

For my punishment homework, I made up the shortest
rhyming lines I could think of:

> Roses are red
>
> Before they are dead.

The next morning, Mrs. Joy, who I'd decided to call
No Joy, tapped her long curved nail on my desk. "Ally
Miller, I believe you have something for me?" she said.

I pulled out my pages of "Roses are red/Before they
are dead," and out fell Tina's note.

"What's this?" Mrs. No Joy pinched the note between
her pincer nails and read out loud to the entire class what
a wonderful world it would be if she swallowed a pencil
and died.

All around me, I heard kids trying not to laugh. Behind me, I heard Tina groaning, waving her arm out of its socket again.

"Tina! Not now!" Mrs. No Joy stared at me so hard I couldn't drop my eyes.

"But Ally didn't write it. I did," Tina shouted out. "Remember we were talking about rhyming lines, and I just wrote it to—"

"Tina Tamblin!" Mrs. No Joy switched her eyes from me to Tina. I looked too, and I couldn't believe what I saw. Tina had done her hair all up like Princess Leia. She kept on talking.

"—be funny."

"Get up here." Mrs. No Joy puckered her lips as she wrote furiously on a piece of paper, then folded it in half. "Since you like notes so much, you can take this one to the principal." She handed Tina the note. Then, as Tina approached the door, Mrs. No Joy nudged my shoulder. "You too."

I made it to the hall before the tears fell.

Tina stopped and stared, but I kept on walking. So

she ran around me and blocked my way, "Please don't cry," she said.

"Shhhh," I said. "You already got us into enough trouble."

"Here." She pulled a tissue out of the pocket of her red corduroy jumper. "I'm sorry I got you in trouble."

It was the first time I noticed that Tina was wearing plaid tights. I never knew there was such a thing as plaid tights.

I blew my nose as our footsteps echoed down the hall.

Tina started talking again and drowned them out. "Don't worry. I'll explain everything to Ms. Creeley. She's really nice. The first day, when my mother brought me to the office 'cause we had to register, Ms. Creeley said, 'I survived the fifth grade and so will you.' She likes me."

"Shhhh," I whispered, then had to add, "Just because she talked to you doesn't mean she likes you."

"My best friend Kirby used to say I was a show-off," Tina whispered back. "She said my head was as big as a blimp. Then I'd say, 'The *Hindenburg*,' and run around like I was putting out a fire on my head."

In the middle of the hall, Tina started running around like she was putting out a fire on her Princess Leia hair. "Do you know about the *Hindenburg?*"

I didn't answer.

"It was like the first giant blimp in the world and it caught on fire," she whispered. "I think it landed on a town and burned some houses down. Back then blimps didn't have message tails like 'Drink Budweiser.' People used to fly in them for fun. Those blimps were as big as football fields. They played football in them too. Wouldn't that be fun, to play football in a blimp?"

"Are you making this up?"

"Only the football part. There really were giant blimps, though, and the *Hindenburg* really did burn up in the sky. Cross my heart." She licked her fingers, then crossed her heart. It left a wet spot. "My grandfather says my imagination will either get me in trouble or make me famous. I'm going to be a reporter and a photographer. What do you want to be?"

I still didn't answer.

When we got to the office, thank you, Lucky Stars, the secretary, Ms. Greenblatt, shushed Tina as soon as she tried to talk. We sat and sat, waiting. Lunch had come and gone by the time Ms. Greenblatt told us to go ahead in.

Ms. Creeley was as tall as a tall man. She was sitting behind her desk holding a pen, which she laid down next to her coffee cup. "Please take a seat," she said.

We sat in front of the big bowl of Hershey's Kisses on her desk. I could smell the chocolate straight through the foil.

"Tina, I'm surprised to see you here," Ms. Creeley said. "And you are Ally Miller, am I right?"

I nodded.

"Now, what got you in trouble?" Ms. Creeley asked.

Like a jack-in-the-box, Tina popped out of her seat and reported the whole story, pacing back and forth like a lawyer in front of a jury on TV. She concluded with, "I know it's rude to write a poem wishing that someone would swallow a pencil and die, but *die* rhymed with

Bye-bye. It was only a joke. Mrs. Joy should learn to laugh. My grandfather says laughing makes you live longer. It's a scientific fact. And Mrs. Joy could use a little help. She's no spring chicken, if you know what I mean."

Ms. Creeley almost smiled. "You do understand it's against school rules to pass notes in class."

"I'm new, so I didn't technically exactly know, but I kind of did. I mean, it's against the rules in my old school. Oh, I almost forgot." Tina handed Ms. Creeley Mrs. Joy's note.

Ms. Creeley read it, then folded it back up. "And Ally, you agree, obviously, that you were an innocent by-stander?"

I nodded.

"Your name is Miller. You're not related to Freddy Miller, are you?"

Me and Freddy Miller, the two juvenile delinquents of East Meadow, New Jersey. "No," I said.

"Who's Freddy Miller?" Just like that, Tina asked what I'd been dying to hear since kindergarten.

"Freddy Miller was a student who went to this school," Ms. Creeley explained, "oh, I don't know, around five years ago. He was quite a memorable young man."

"Why? What did he do?" Tina sat up straight to hear the story. I did too.

"That's for another time. Right now, I have to decide what to do with you. Ally, Mrs. Joy thinks you should be punished, but I don't agree. I'm curious, what do you think Tina's punishment should be?"

"To write 'I will not pass notes in class' one hundred times?"

Ms. Creeley didn't seem to like the idea, so I said, "Peel potatoes in the cafeteria?"

"I think I have a better idea," Ms. Creeley said. "Why don't you write a poem, Tina? Come to think of it, why don't you write one, too, Ally? I know that you don't deserve to be punished, but I'm not considering this a punishment. I'm considering it a challenge, if you'd like to take it on."

I wanted to show Ms. Creeley I could do it, so I said, "Sure."

"That's what I like to hear. Then it's settled. You'll both write me a poem. Let's see." She looked at her calendar. "I'll give you a week. Please bring it to me next Monday."

"Ms. Creeley," Tina said. "I was wondering, could we have one of those Hershey's Kisses?"

I thought you were supposed to wait till you were offered, that asking was rude. But Ms. Creeley said, "Help yourself," and offered Tina the bowl. And then she offered it to me, too. "Take a few."

Tina took a whole handful, so I did too.

* Chapter Eight *

That week, the hall monitors were chosen. Guess who got to answer Ms. Creeley's phone during lunch period three days a week? Betsy. Guess who wasn't even chosen to clean the blackboards? Me.

Betsy began bringing her guitar to school, and during recess she and her band sang Beatles songs. Meanwhile, every day at lunch Tina had a different bad idea for the talent show to share with George and Karl and me.

"We should do what my best friend Kirby and I did in my backyard for the earthquake relief fund for South America," she suggested on Friday. "Ventriloquism. I tied my stuffed monkey, Philip, to my shoulder, then tucked his arm into my hair band to make him sit up. I made my mouth look like it kind of might be talking, but really it was Kirby behind a tree with a microphone. I said, 'So, Philip, how you doing?' And Philip said, 'Give me a banana.' I said, 'So, Philip, how do you like being a monkey?' And Philip said, 'Give me a banana.' That's all he ever said, no matter what I asked him. So finally Arpie, this five-year-old, threw him a whole bunch of bananas, and that was the end. It was a comedy."

None of us laughed.

✳

By Saturday morning, I still hadn't written a word of my poem for Ms. Creeley. Bored of trying, I stepped outside to get the paper to read the funnies and saw Mona drive by with Betsy and her mother. I bet they were going to Betsy's aunt Alma's house in Connecticut. Aunt Alma had chickens and ducks and served tea in china cups on a screened-in porch.

Thinking about all I was missing, I stepped back inside, dropped the paper on the kitchen table, and headed for my room. I sat at my desk, opened my notebook, and wrote a poem so fast it was like it had already existed. It was about Betsy and me—and so private, I'd never show it to a single soul.

I read it over, and as the wind rattled my window, I sat up taller to look outside at the trees in our yard. There are two of them—a weeping willow whose branches sweep the ground like a curtain, and a big old oak whose branches reach way higher than our roof into the sky.

Suddenly I felt an urge to run outside. When I reached the oak tree, the wind was blowing its branches so they looked like Beethoven's hair in a storm. At the other edge of the yard, the willow branches swayed back and forth, and I ran through them like they were a curtain. No one could see me under the willow tent unless they were looking. When the branches swayed, so did I. I leapt in a circle around the trunk, I twirled on my toes, I fell onto my knees and waved my arms like tree branches. I rolled onto my back. I kicked my feet in the air and then my hands, too. I made my arms and legs open and close, bend and curl, slowly and gracefully, until they were doing a dance on their own—until they were turtle arms and legs and my body was the shell. And when I was completely exhausted, I got up, brushed myself off, and walked peacefully back to my room.

✳

There was a full moon that night, and my room was as dark as a shadow. From bed, I could see my doll, Katie, sitting on the bureau. She was named after my sister, who'd died fifteen years ago, before I was born. I never played with dolls anymore, but Katie looked awfully lonely over there, so I got out of bed to tuck her in with me.

Back in bed, I sat her on my lap. Out the window, I could see the Man in the Moon looking down. I thought how a moonbeam aimed straight at me might be the same as being touched by a magic wand, and then I imagined that Katie said hi. Only she wasn't my doll anymore, she was my sister. That really spooked me so I laid her down quickly to make her eyes close. But then I felt so sad never to have known my real sister, I lay down next to Katie and hugged her tight.

Nodding off to sleep a few minutes later, I thought of the first line for my poem for Ms. Creeley and woke right up. I turned on the light, reached over to my desk for my notebook, propped it on my knees, and wrote the whole thing in about two minutes.

✳ Chapter Nine ✳

On the front page of the *East Meadow Eagle* the next morning there was a picture of Ruby, Betsy and Mona's band. Betsy was on the left wearing a hair band, strumming her guitar, Charlie sat in back at the drums, and Gracie was on the right playing keyboard. In the middle, in a miniskirt and holding a microphone with both hands, was Mona. Under the picture it said, "Look for Ruby at Heady Hollow's Annual Fifth-Grade Talent Show."

I thought how green is the color for envy, and took off the green shirt I'd been wearing. And then I took off my jeans and put on a miniskirt of my own. I also dug out a pocketbook from the top of my closet, a hand-me-down from my cousin Francesca. It was white plastic with a big orange daisy on it.

That's why I was carrying my books in my arms instead of in a backpack when Artie and Stu ran into me on my way into school. I dropped everything. "Excuse me, excuse me. Sorry, sorry, so sorry," they joked, jostling me and kicking my books all over the sidewalk. When I tried to pick them up, other kids kicked them farther away. Then I saw Mona put her foot on one of my papers and my mouth started to tremble. Before I could even try to stop them, tears squirted from my eyes. "I hate you!" I yelled.

"Oh, no! Ally Miller hates me!" Artie clutched at his heart.

I'd said it to Mona, not him.

"I think I'm going to cry." He pretend-cried so loud, Mr. Watson, a fourth-grade teacher, came over. "What's going on?" he said.

Nobody answered, and neither did I. "What did they do to you?" Mr. Watson asked. "Are you all right?"

I nodded.

"Why don't you go to the girls' room and wash your face?" He put his hand on my shoulder and guided me into the building. My books and papers were still scattered everywhere.

I ran down the hall into the lavatory. Inside a stall, I clamped my hands over my mouth so nobody could hear me sobbing. I couldn't understand why I was the big target. Why was everyone so mean to me? And what would I tell Mrs. Joy had happened to my homework, my books? We weren't supposed to fold down even one tiny corner of one single page. And what about my poem for Ms. Creeley?

I stepped out of the stall and splashed water on my face. As I dabbed it dry with paper towels, I heard the lavatory door start to open and dashed back into the stall.

"Ally?" It was Tina. "That was the meanest thing I've ever seen."

I was afraid to talk in case I started crying all over again.

"I got your books and most of your papers," she said.

"Thank you." I was *so* relieved.

"Are you coming out? We're going to be late."

I stepped back out of the stall.

"Here." She handed me my books in a neat pile. "I told that kid Artie he was a Neanderthal. You know what he did? Scratched his armpits like an ape." She laughed, then held the door open for me.

Even though Tina's collecting my books might have been the nicest thing anyone had ever done for me, I have to admit, I really didn't want to be walking with her. Especially when I heard a girl say to her, "May the Force be with you." Tina's hair was like Princess Leia's again.

"And with you," Tina answered.

✳

In class, Mrs. No Joy announced to Tina and me that we were to go see Ms. Creeley after lunch. I tore my poem out of my notebook and folded it in half. Thank you, Lucky Stars, Artie and Stu hadn't gotten their paws on it.

Tina and I left lunch a little early. Just as we reached the office door, Betsy stepped out, still talking to Ms.

Creeley. I heard Ms. Creeley say, "Now all you need's a go-go dancer."

"I know, right?" Betsy turned with a big smile on her face, which she didn't take off when she saw me and Tina.

"Hi," Tina said.

So I said hi too.

And Betsy actually said hi back!

Ms. Creeley invited us in, then leaned back in her chair, put her feet up on her desk, and said, "I can't think of a better way to start the week. Who'd like to read her poem first?"

Tina raised her hand. She stood in front of the tall window. "Mine doesn't rhyme. It's free form," she said. And she began.

> "When autumn comes
> The leaves turn red and orange and
>   yellow
> Until they flutter and fly and
>   eventually die.

The grass turns brown,

The days shrink,

The snows fall.

Then one day a bird sings,

The snow melts,

The grass turns green,

And the baby buds on trees burst

Into big fat leaves until

They turn red and orange and yellow."

Tina bowed.

"It's very nice the way it ends back where it began. The form's called circular," said Ms. Creeley.

"I didn't plan it that way," said Tina. "It just came out."

"I like it a lot."

Ms. Creeley looked at me, "And Ally?"

"Mine rhymes. It's short."

"Good. Let's hear it."

I stood in front of the window too.

"Once there was a man in the moon.

Everyone thought he was a scary old loon.

But when I waved, he winked at me,

And so I invited him in for tea.

He was the loneliest man in the sky

But down on Earth we ate pie."

I was afraid to look up, until, thank you, Lucky Stars, Tina clapped and Ms. Creeley said, "Very touching. The moon is all alone, no one likes him, but one person made all the difference. Nice work."

"I always think he looks like he's winking too," Tina said.

"That was a treat; thank you, girls." Ms. Creeley lifted her legs off her desk.

"Ms. Creeley, I've been thinking," Tina said. "Those bulletin boards advertising the talent show seem awfully plain. Shouldn't they have some pictures? My mother's an artist. She could draw them."

"If she'd agree to do that, Tina, I think that would

be wonderful. So, are you going to perform in the show?"

"We haven't decided yet," Tina told her.

"You're doing something together?"

I said, "No," at the same time Tina said, "Maybe."

"You're doing something alone?" Ms. Creeley asked me.

"I'm not going to be in the talent show," I told her.

"Ally, that's a shame," said Ms. Creeley. "Let me explain something to you. The reason we began this tradition is because of the annual show at my own elementary school. Back in the fifth grade, I was shy and didn't want to perform either. But a very astute teacher pressured me into it and I don't think it's an exaggeration to say it changed my life. A wise man once said, 'Always do what you fear to do most.' "

"There's nothing to fear but fear itself," Tina threw in. "My grandfather says that when I'm afraid to do stuff like jump in the ocean from his boat."

"Franklin Delano Roosevelt." Ms. Creeley nodded.

I wouldn't have been afraid at all if I were going to be

in the show with Betsy. Especially since her singing always drowned mine out. But obviously I couldn't tell Ms. Creeley and Tina that, so I just sat there.

"Do you want me to believe you have no special something you like to do when you're alone in your room—no special talent?" Ms. Creeley crossed her leg and pumped her foot. That's when I noticed how big her feet were. "Because I find that hard to believe."

Now she turned to Tina. "Tina, would you please excuse us? Ally and I have a little matter to discuss."

"Sure." Tina stood. "See you." She held up her palm, then walked out the door.

Ms. Creeley looked gently at me. "Ally, honey, Mr. Watson told me that you were crying this morning, and he escorted you to the lav. Would you like to tell me what you were upset about?"

I wanted to drip into a puddle and evaporate.

"If you could help me understand what the problem is, I might be able to help you."

I couldn't tell her. It was too embarrassing.

"Ally, look at me."

I looked at her—well, really I looked at her mouth. My eyes filled with tears.

Ms. Creeley handed me a tissue. "What happened, dear?"

"I can't tell you. I'd be a tattletale."

"Fair enough. Then don't tell me the other kids' names."

I stared at her big feet and thought how she was almost freakishly tall. Ms. Creeley might understand what it felt like to be picked on. Plus, not telling her was beginning to seem rude. "Two boys bumped into me," I admitted, "and then I dropped my books and they kicked them all over the place."

"Is there a reason for those two boys to bully you?"

"They hate me. They were trying to make me cry."

"And you don't want to tell me who these boys are?"

I shook my head.

"They've made you cry before?"

"Yes."

"Well, it seems to me you have to find some way to not let them get to you."

"I know."

"When I get upset, I breathe very deeply. Way down in my belly. It's a relaxation technique I learned from yoga. It calms me right down. Why don't you try it?"

"Now?" I asked.

"Why not?" said Ms. Creeley. "Close your eyes and breathe through your nose."

I tried it.

"Now imagine that your belly is a balloon and breathe air into it."

I did.

"Good. Blow it up really big, really puff it out, then exhale, slowly, letting the air out through your nose."

I followed everything she was saying. And it did make me feel calmer.

"How was that?"

"Good."

"Ally." Ms. Creeley shifted in her chair. "I have to tell you, I've noticed you sitting by yourself in the cafeteria— off in the corner. Sometimes in life, for whatever reason, we isolate ourselves. Maybe we feel that no one likes us, or we have no friends. That's exactly when we have to try extra hard to extend ourselves, take a risk, get involved."

I nodded, wishing with all my heart Ms. Creeley would finally dismiss me.

"You know what's coming next, don't you?"

"No," I said.

"I think you should perform in the talent show. It really doesn't matter if you're good or not—it's all in the spirit of fun. Performing is therapeutic. Believe me, Ally, it's just what the doctor ordered. Will you promise me to at least think about it?"

"Okay."

"Okay, good." Ms. Creeley stood up. "Let's shake on it, shall we?"

We shook.

* Chapter Ten *

Here are the times I cried in public before this year:

—My first day of kindergarten, because my mother left me and I was scared.

—In the first grade in art when we were drawing a bird. The teacher and the rest of the class were already on the tail while I was still on the wing.

Then I didn't cry in school again—all through second and third and fourth grades—until the first day of school this year when Betsy dumped me.

Since then, it seemed like I'd cried almost every day—which was really embarrassing, which made me cry more.

Crying in public is not acceptable.

The worst thing is not being able to control it.

I had to stop.

Lying on my bed after school, I closed my eyes and concentrated hard, willing myself never to cry in public again.

I decided to practice the breathing thing Ms. Creeley had taught me. As I filled up my belly like a balloon, I remembered how Tina had told me Ms. Creeley liked her and I hadn't believed her. But it was true: Ms. Creeley did like Tina. And she liked me, too. Ms. Creeley really wanted me to be in the talent show. Shouldn't I give it a try? But what could I possibly do?

Of course, I could always do something lame with Tina, but that would be as bad as spinning in front of the class without underwear.

The only thing I really knew how to do was dance. But I could never dance alone, and besides, Ms. Janet, my one and only dancing teacher, had thought I was terrible. Then my mother had said I was great at rock and roll, just not ballet. I knew all the dances from the sixties and seventies, from my parents' day, because my parents had danced with me in the kitchen since before I could walk.

Betsy's mother had even asked me to teach her to disco once.

I remembered a tutu in my closet that I'd bought at a yard sale. It was white and fluffy like a hundred thousand floating feathers. I dug it out of the closet, then slipped off my jeans and pulled it on. Standing on my bed, I looked in the mirror above my bureau. I rose onto my toes like a ballerina, then ever so gently began to jump up and down, watching the layers float up to my elbows, then fall back down. I did the jerk, and as I watched the tutu shiver, I was struck so hard by my brilliant idea I fell backward.

I should go-go dance with Betsy's band! I'd overheard Ms. Creeley tell Betsy that her band should have a go-go dancer. And then Betsy had smiled and said hi to me. Maybe she'd been thinking the same thing. I was a natural and Betsy knew it. I was so excited, I started to vibrate. What did I have to lose? I would just ask her. There was nothing to fear but fear itself, right?

I hugged myself and lay there, planning it all out. I'd sit with Betsy and her band at lunch. Maybe I'd even like

Mona and start blowing my hair too. We'd rehearse every day with Charlie and Gracie. A talent scout would come to the talent show and single out me and Betsy to star in a huge Hollywood movie about two best friends who discover they're really sisters. And then they become rock stars together.

All I had to do was ask.

I sat up, filled up my stomach with air, then exhaled as I dialed the phone. When her mother answered, I asked for Betsy.

"Ally?" she said. "What a nice surprise. It's been a long time. How are you?"

"Fine," I said. "I've been dancing a lot."

"Good. Look, honey, Betsy's not here. Shall I tell her you called?"

"Thanks. And would you tell her to call me back?"

"Certainly."

＊

I stayed up late waiting for Betsy to call. But she never did.

✳

At the bus stop the next morning, I couldn't ask Betsy about being Ruby's go-go dancer in front of everybody, especially Mona. But it was only a half day, so I wouldn't have to wait long. I'd call her as soon as I got home.

We only studied four subjects, but it felt like ten. After school on the bus line, Tina bumped her shoulder into mine. "This your bus?"

"Yeah."

"I'm taking it too." Tina was a walker. She wasn't even supposed to be in line.

"You can't do that," I told her.

"It's only once, for a ride. Don't you love buses? I wish it were a double-decker. In some places in the world where there are too many people and it doesn't rain, they even have a third story up on the roof. Wouldn't that be heaven?"

"You can't just ride the bus. The bus driver won't let you."

"I'm good at blending in. He won't notice. I have to

71

see the town. I don't even know where the garbage dump is. Is there a skating rink?"

"They turned it into a Wal-Mart. The one-hour photo place is where you used to rent your skates."

Tina was right. Lenny, the bus driver, didn't say a word.

I sat in the front seat, as usual. Tina, of course, sat next to me, and then patted the seat for George to sit with us, three in a seat.

As soon as we started to move, Artie called out, "Anybody want to hear a poem?"

"Noooo!" kids screamed back. "Boooo! Maggots! Barf!"

"By the famous poet"—he paused—"AAAALL-LLYYYYY THEEEEERRRRREEEEESAAAA MIIIIL-LLER!"

How could he have gotten my Man in the Moon poem? It was like a nightmare come true.

Kids bounced in their seats. Clapped their hands. Stomped their feet.

"Quiet back there!" Lenny scowled into his wide rearview mirror.

Everyone quieted down.

Artie waited half a minute, then began, making his voice high like a girl's.

I remembered the poem as soon as he started. It was the private one I'd written about Betsy. I must have left it loose in my notebook and it had fallen out.

Betsy and Mona were a few rows behind me. I could actually feel them listening. I squeezed my eyes shut, breathing deeply, telling myself, *Don't cry. Don't cry. Don't cry.*

"Once we rode our bikes and dreamed
   on the grass together.
Once I slept over her house and in bed
   we giggled together.
Once we made mud pies.
Once we pushed our dolls in strollers.
Once we sang songs on a swing.

Once we would be best friends forever.

Now she rides bikes, dreams on the grass,

   and giggles with someone else.

Now I am alone.

Now I have no friend.

When will the loneliness end?"

I kept my eyes squeezed tight and remembered to fill my stomach with air again.

"Boo-hoo, wah-wah, Ally has no friends," Artie pretend-cried, and then it seemed like the whole bus was pretend-crying with him.

"*Quiet!*" Lenny yelled.

Everyone pretend-cried more quietly.

I sneaked a look back at Betsy. She was laughing hysterically with Mona.

"Excuse me." Tina stood in the aisle and faced the whole bus.

"Sit down!" Lenny said into his rearview mirror.

She sat, then kneeled on her seat, facing the crowd. "I have an announcement to make."

"I have an announcement to make," Artie imitated.

"Silence." Tina glared at him. "This is the announcement. Please spread the news: Artie Kaminsky's parents tried to give him back at the hospital when the doctors showed them an X-ray of his brain. And they discovered it was a cow plop. Go ahead, Artie. Repeat it."

The kids laughed.

"Repeat after me, Artie Kaminsky has a cow plop brain."

"Artie Kaminsky has a cow plop brain!" the whole bus yelled.

Lenny banged the steering wheel. "Simmer down!"

Everyone simmered down.

Staring out the window, I knew that I could never ask to go-go dance now.

Tina tapped me on the shoulder. "That poem was about your best friend?" she asked me.

I nodded.

"Betsy," George explained. He'd known us since kindergarten.

"The Betsy who's in our class? And now she's best

friends with that blond girl I always see her with?" Tina asked.

"Mona." I told her how Mona had stolen Betsy away from me. Then I told her how Artie Kaminsky had stolen my rhinestone clip and given it to Mona.

"I've sent my best friend Kirby three cards, two letters, and a picture of me holding a sign that says 'Write Me.' And she never writes back. But I guess it's worse if you see your best friend all the time and she's best friends with somebody else."

I nodded. "It stinks."

"Hey, but maybe Betsy's sorry. Maybe you'll make up."

For the first time, I knew that wasn't true. "She can't stand me," I said.

"I'll be your friend," Tina said quietly.

And I realized that maybe she already was.

★ Chapter Eleven ★

You know those lines in the wedding vows, "For better or for worse, in sickness and in health"? When I thought about it, I saw how that was kind of how it would feel being friends with Tina—except for the "till death do us part" part. Here was the "worse" part: she really did look like she had a pet snake, and she did sometimes wear weird Princess Leia hair. She talked All The Time, and kept right on waving her arm like a rusty fan in class even though Mrs. No Joy hardly ever called on her. And Tina was a reject.

Then again, so was I.

Here was the "better" part: she was funny in her strange Tina way. She was really smart and knew a lot about a whole lot of things, even if she did make some of it up. And she liked me, even though she could plainly see that just about nobody else did. Plus, she'd stuck up for me. She was a loyal friend. And I had to admit, lunchtime was the most fun part of every day.

And so when Tina invited me to her house after school to cut out pictures for the talent show bulletin boards, I accepted.

Her house was next to the 7-Eleven, with a parking lot for a front yard. It was so tiny you wouldn't notice it behind the chain-link fence unless you were looking for it. The porch was slanted and the one big window at the front made the house look like it had a missing tooth.

The door wasn't locked. The second we walked in, I knew I'd never seen a house like Tina's, not even in a movie. The living room was painted bright pink with lime green surrounding the windows. The only furniture was a mattress on the floor, covered by a piece of fabric with little striped fish all over it and one red rose-shaped pillow. Mirrors in different sizes and shapes and frames covered a whole wall. A round table was crowded with cans of brushes and tubes of paint. On an easel sat a painting of Tina with a monkey on her shoulder.

"Philip," she said when she noticed me staring at it. "He's stuffed, remember I told you about him in that show I did with Kirby? Do you know what trompe l'oeil is? When you paint a window or something on a wall to look like it's real? Like if it's a window, you think you're looking out it at the lawn and the trees, but it's just a painting? That's what my mother usually paints. My mother says she's an illusionist. She also works for a publisher designing book covers from home. She's supposed to be here. "MA!" Tina yelled. "We're here!"

Tina had told me that her mother was going to draw pictures that we'd trace onto construction paper, then cut out.

"Who's 'we'?" Her mother walked in barefoot, looking like she'd just woken up. Her long curly hair was the color of cranberry sauce and all messed up.

"Me and Ally," Tina said. "Mom, this is Ally. She's going to help me cut out the pictures. Did you draw them?"

"Tina." Her mother placed her hand on her heart. "You have a school friend. I'm so happy for you."

"Mom, where are the pictures?"

"They'll only take me a minute. . . . Ally—what a nice name. Is it short for Alexandra or Alfreda? Or did your mother wish you were a boy, and when she saw that you were a girl, change Allen to Ally?"

"It's just Ally, like an alley without the *e*."

"Did you know Tina means *sink* in Spanish?" Tina asked.

"Tina is named after her great-grandmother Valentina. I think I should have named her Valentina, don't you?"

I thought Tina should thank her Lucky Stars her mother hadn't.

"My name is Marta, short for Martian. Only kidding."

I thought Martian kind of fit.

Tina's mom drew us a musical note, a trumpet, a dancing bear, drums, and those sad and happy masks from drama. Then we took them out to the porch to trace onto different-colored construction paper.

We sat on the top step, and after we'd been working for around a half hour, a little girl walked over.

"Lulu!" Tina said. "What's shakin'?"

Lulu turned around and shook her fanny.

I had a feeling that was their routine.

"This is my friend Ally," Tina said after Lulu turned back around.

"Hi," Lulu said. She must have been in preschool or kindergarten. She reminded me of a cute little mouse. Her hair was brown like mine, but her eyes were speckled blue and green and brown. She was wearing a blue flowered dress with a yellow sweater that was too big. "Can I cut some out too?" she asked Tina.

I thought she was awfully young to use scissors. But Tina said, "Sure. Have a seat."

Lulu sat between us. Tina handed her a scissors and a page of trumpets on orange construction paper, then disappeared back into the house for more scissors.

Lulu said, "Trumpets," as she placed the paper on her lap and began cutting.

In about a second, Lulu dropped her scissors, stood

and stared at her dress. She'd cut straight through the construction paper and made a big hole in the skirt. She kind of froze for a few seconds, then started marching her feet in place, waving her hands by her ears and crying really loudly, like she was being attacked by a swarm of bees.

"Don't worry." I stood too. "It was an accident," I said as Tina came running out.

"What happened?" she asked.

I told Tina, "She cut her dress."

"Boo!" Tina jumped at Lulu, and it worked like stopping hiccups, only Lulu switched from crying to giggling. Then, as soon as she managed to stop, she took her dress off. Her undershirt and underpants had little bunnies all over them.

For some reason, Tina saluted and started singing "Yankee Doodle." They probably sang it all the time, and it kind of made me wish I was their neighbor. I love that song. It's in an old movie with an actor in it named Jimmy Cagney, who usually plays gangsters. In the movie he marches so fast and stiff-legged while tap-dancing at the same time that he looks like a tin soldier with ants in his pants.

I imitated Jimmy Cagney march-tap-dancing down the steps; then Tina and Lulu imitated me, and the next thing I knew, they were following me around the house like Simon Says, with Lulu in her underwear. It was kind of cold out, but nobody cared.

✳

On the weekend, I wanted to call Tina and ask her to come over, but I didn't have her phone number and she wasn't listed in the phone book. Instead, I decided to wash my father's truck and to ask Sissy, the six-year-old pest, if she wanted to help. If Tina could be friends with a little kid, maybe I could be nicer to the little kid I knew.

When I saw Sissy playing in her yard, I called out to her. "Wanna help me give this a bath?" and I pointed at the truck. Sissy didn't even answer. She ran home to ask permission and returned looking like an advertisement for rain. She had put on a yellow slicker and red rubber boots and was holding a giant sponge. "I'll wash the tires," she said.

When she'd finished one tire, she wanted the hose. "I need to rinse it," she said.

"Sorry, that's my job," I told her. Squirting the suds off is the most fun about washing a truck. The best thing about playing with little kids is you get to be the boss.

Once the outside of the truck was finished, I had a brilliant idea. I dumped the whole bucket of suds into the truck bed and draped the hose over the truck's side so it gushed water, then jumped in, marching stiff-legged like a *Nutcracker* soldier. Sissy imitated me, and pretty soon, just like in *Singin' in the Rain,* we were splashing up a storm.

At that moment, Tina rode up on her bicycle, hit the brakes, and spun in a circle.

"I wanted to call you!" I said.

"I got your vibes!" she said, hopping into the truck bed too. "Hey!" She kicked in the middle of twirling. "This is like *Singin' in the Rain.*"

"Exactly!" I shouted, and twirled just like her. We marched. We skipped. We skated. We stood on the truck sides and jumped down. Then Sissy picked up the hose and squirted us, and we screamed, which made my father appear on the porch.

"Girls, girls, girls, what do you think this is, a party? Your mother needs some quiet, okay, peanuts for brains?"

Whenever he called me that, I always answered, "Liver for dinner," which I did now. It cracked Tina up.

We sat in the cab of the truck. I took the driver's seat, Tina took the passenger's side, and Sissy rested her butt in the middle of the backseat and stuck her head between us.

"You should meet Lulu," Tina said to Sissy. "She's five."

"I'm six. My name's Sissy."

"Are you called Sissy because you're a sister?" Tina asked.

"No. Because my real name is Melissa and my cousin couldn't pronounce 'Missy.' She said 'Sissy.' "

"My name's Tina and I'm not a sister either."

"Me neither," I chimed in. I didn't tell them about Katie. "If you could drive anywhere in the United States, where would you go?"

"Disney World," said Sissy.

"I'd go to Rock Island, where my grandfather lives," Tina said. "You have to take a ferry, and there are no cars. In the summer there are lots of people, but in the winter hardly anyone stays. You can sit on practically any porch and nobody cares. The wind howls like a bunch of ghosts. If there's a hurricane, the sea comes right up to my grandfather's door.

"You should see, there's this one beach with about ten thousand seagulls. If you go there real late in the afternoon, you can see them all facing the same direction, standing on one foot, watching the sun go down. My grandfather says it's like when people stand up for the National Anthem. It's a ritual, only for seagulls."

"That's funny," I said, deciding right then I wanted to go.

"I'll probably go there for the summer," Tina went on. "My grandfather likes kids. He says he doesn't want to die like this poet from South America, who said his biggest regret was that he didn't talk to more kids."

Sissy burst out fake laughing the way little kids do when they're trying to sound grown-up.

"What's so funny?" I asked her.

"Talking to kids."

"Oh, you're going to love Lulu," Tina said.

Pretty soon it was almost dark. My mother called me in, Sissy went home, and Tina rode off before I realized I still didn't have her phone number.

✳ Chapter Twelve ✳

The whole next week, Tina didn't come to school. Now it was Friday morning, and Ms. Creeley was announcing over the intercom that the talent show had turned into a talent *contest*. This year, for the first time, fifth grades in schools across the state were having talent contests. A video of each winning act was to be entered into a statewide competition. Judges from Channel 7 would select the top ten acts, then broadcast videos of them on a special show on February 28. Viewers would call in to select one winning act, who would get five hundred dollars, plus a trip to Atlantic City for the awards ceremony.

A student from East Meadow High was going to produce the video of the winning act from our talent show.

And Tina didn't even know.

The first day she didn't come to school, I'd figured

she had something normal like a cold or a stomachache, but it had been almost a week and I was afraid she was sick with a real disease like chicken pox. She might even have had her tonsils taken out—which would mean she'd miss being in the talent show. The deadline for signing up was next Friday, only one week away!

Every day I'd been walking by Ms. Wiley the music teacher's door where the sign-up sheet was posted—just to keep track of who was in the show. That morning, I walked by it again. Betsy, Mona, Charlie, and Gracie, of course, had signed up as "Band." Lizzy and Vicki Adams, who were twins, signed up as "Tap Dance." Mitsy Patrick would twirl her baton, and Barbara Harrison would play her accordion. Artie and Stu were down for Tae Kwon Do. There were skits, a rapper, acrobats, one ballet dancer, a juggler, one cello player, one clarinet player, and two piano players. More than ever, not being in the talent show felt like looking through a window at somebody else's Christmas.

If Tina were in school, smoke would be pouring out her pop-out ears from all the ideas she'd be cooking up for the show. I was actually a little disappointed I didn't get to hear what she would come up with. What if one of the ideas was good?

The whole school was so excited it was a different place, like a prison turned into a park. In the lunch line the Adams twins did a shuffle-ball-change tap, Betsy's band burst into song, and Artie and Stu kicked at each other, which made Mr. Korn, the lunch monitor, jam his hands on his hips and say, "Everybody, straighten up!"

I'd worn chopsticks in my hair like I'd seen Natalie Portman do in *People* magazine. As soon as Mr. Korn looked the other way, Artie pulled them out, gave one to Stu, and they sword-fought with them. I pretended the chopsticks weren't even mine. (They were just from takeout, anyway.) I got my sloppy joe, then sat at the middle of the table with George and Karl. I sat with them every day now. It had been less than two weeks, but it felt like we'd been talking for centuries.

Today Karl asked, "Do you watch *The Devil Take You?*"

It was a really silly show, a bunch of skits these high school kids improvised about screwing up badly. It came on our local cable channel once a week. "It's my favorite show!" I said. I didn't know anyone else watched it.

Karl high-fived me. "The kid with the thick glasses is a genius. If it's still on when we're in high school, I'm doing special effects for it. I'm getting this new program for my Mac. It's state-of-the-art."

"I'm worried about Tina." I changed the subject to what I'd been thinking about all morning. "Do you think she's got a disease or something? She's going to miss the talent show deadline."

"Did she tell you she was going to do a magic act?" Karl asked.

"What magic?" George asked.

"That's what I said." Karl tilted so far back in his chair I thought he'd tip over. "The usual, she said. Pulling a rabbit out of a hat, scarves out of sleeves."

"Do you think she can really do that?" I asked.

"All I know is if George here would enter the show, he'd win. But he's too chicken."

George looked so far up with his eyeballs they looked like Ping-Pong balls.

"His mother wants him to be in the show, but he won't. Ask him why."

"Why?" I asked George.

George licked the sides of his ice cream sandwich and said nothing.

Once in the fourth grade, I'd heard George play. I'd been sick and he'd brought my homework to me. As usual, he'd had his violin, and my mother asked if he'd play us something. He'd bent his knees and closed his eyes, and when he played he looked like he was listening to a heaven full of angels singing, only he was the one making the music. My whole body had flooded with goose bumps.

"Oh, c'mon, why won't you?" I asked again.

George swallowed, wiped his mouth with his napkin, and got up to leave.

I wondered how he could not want the whole school to see how talented he was.

*

On the bus going home, I sat in the front seat next to George and his violin, and he smiled at me.

"If your mother told you you could quit and you never had to play the violin again, would you still play?" I asked.

"I don't know. Probably."

"Could you play since you were little?"

"Since I was two."

"Don't you think it's lucky to be born with talent?"

"Maybe."

"What's not lucky about it?"

"Responsibility."

I didn't know what he meant by that and he didn't explain, so I asked him, "What responsibility?"

"I'm supposed to *use* it when I grow up. I couldn't just be a skateboarder or something."

I'd been thinking that George was lucky to be so talented, but I guess sometimes there's a bit of unlucky in lucky. That made me wonder if there's also a bit of lucky in unlucky.

While we'd been talking, I'd noticed that the bus had grown unusually quiet.

Suddenly Artie yelled, "Bombs away!" Spitballs flew from behind, covering George's and my shoulders and piling up in our laps.

George just looked at me and shrugged.

I shrugged back.

✳ Chapter Thirteen ✶

I waited the whole weekend. Then when Tina was still absent Monday, I rode my bike to her house after school and knocked on her door. Thank you, Lucky Stars, I heard running feet, and there was Tina with wet hair stuck behind her pop-out ears. She didn't look very sick. Her jeans were rolled up and she was wearing pink and yellow striped socks and no shoes. Her arms were so long they practically reached her knees. I noticed because they flew into the air in a cheerleader jump. "It's YOU!" she said.

"Aren't you sick?"

"Not really. Well, I was, kind of. I mean, I couldn't come to school. Cross my heart." She licked her fingers and crossed it. "Want some cake? There's a whole cake from a bakery, just delivered. You know how you're never supposed to open the door to strangers? If I followed the exact rule, I couldn't open the door for the deliveryman. But my grandfather says he never met a rule that couldn't be broken, and I had to see what was in the box. Good thing. 'Cause it was a CAKE."

I thought of a rule that can't be broken: Thou Shalt Not Kill. But then I remembered mosquitoes.

The cake was as big as a hat box. It had swirly white frosting with a heart made of real roses in the middle. Tina sliced me a big piece. It was pink inside.

"Is it somebody's birthday?"

"Kind of. Not really. Don't worry. It's okay. We can eat it."

We lifted plates out of the dish drain. The sink was filled with dirty dishes, and the counters were a mess. "We can eat in the living room," she said.

"Where's your mother?" I asked as we sat on the mattress.

"Painting."

"Where?" The table was empty of paints but piled with clothes that still had their price tags on them.

"I think she's painting a mural on the side of a sky-scraper or something. I think it's a trompe l'oeil of a forest."

"Really?"

She nodded, and I wondered if she'd made that up. She was lucky to be home alone without her mother. But the place was so messy. And would her mother really have left Tina alone if she was sick?

We ate with our fingers. The cake was delicious—cherry with chocolate between the layers.

"So were you sick or weren't you?" I asked her.

"I was but now I'm not. I'm recovered. I'm coming back to school tomorrow."

"Tina!" I'd forgotten the news. I told her all about the statewide competition.

"Yahoo!" She jumped on the mattress.

"And the winner gets five hundred dollars!"

She grabbed her heart and fell back on the mattress.

"But you haven't signed up yet," I reminded her.

"I know," she said, sitting up. "Let's do something together please, please, *please*? I really want to do a magic act! I have this huge doll. We could saw her in half. Then when we pull her up to stand, everyone would expect it to be a trick, and that she'd be whole. But it would just be her top half. It's a comedy! Everything we do could go wrong. You could go to pull a rabbit out of a hat, and it's a dead rat."

I groaned. I couldn't believe I'd thought Tina might come up with something I'd actually do.

When we finished eating, we put our plates on the floor next to the mattress. Tina asked if I wanted to listen to music, then pushed the shuffle button on her mother's iPod.

"Eleanor Rigby" by the Beatles started playing. It had a beautiful violin and told a sad story about "all the lonely people." It reminded me of what it was like to be all alone without a friend. I wondered if Tina was thinking the same thing.

Then a jazz song without words blasted on like a storm. We sat there for half a minute and I just couldn't stand it. I wanted to heebie-jeebie something fierce but was afraid Tina would think I'd gone insane. The music tickled my body so badly, it actually hurt not to move.

I stood and Tina stood up too. Tina held her arms out like a cross and ran to the kitchen and back. I closed my eyes and the next thing I knew I was heebie-jeebie-ing like my clothes were on fire.

Every once in a while Tina would run past looking like a dragonfly. It was so cool. She'd gone almost as wild as I had.

Then the song "Disco Fever" came on and I asked Tina if she'd ever heard of *Saturday Night Fever*.

"Is that a song?"

"Oh, my God. It's only the greatest disco movie ever. It's from the seventies. Oh, my God." I bounced against a wall with my shoulder. "It's So Great!" Then I fell onto the mattress facedown and had a brilliant idea. We could disco in the talent show!

"Do you disco?" I asked Tina.

"No." She fell on top of me, tickling my armpits. I tried to reach her feet but I was too spastic from laughing.

We were laughing so hard we didn't hear Tina's

mother walk in the back door. "Tina, Tina, Popina!" she sang from the kitchen.

Tina sat up, looking a little nervous. "Here, Mom."

Her mother walked in like she was wading through mud. She was wearing green rubber boots and a pink bathrobe. I wondered if Tina was as surprised as I was or if she'd known all along that her mother wasn't at a job but off somewhere being totally weird.

"Been down at the pond," Tina's mother said. "Turtles make the best stepping-stones, don't you think?"

I laughed, but Tina didn't.

"You won't find it so funny the next time you need to keep your feet dry." Tina's mother flipped her hair over her shoulder and walked out of the room.

"Did you go to Laurel Pond?" I called out to her. It was the only pond I knew.

"Who?" She came back peeling off her robe. Under it she was wearing a tight black dress with a diamond and pearl necklace.

"Laurel Pond," I repeated.

"She's not the sister of Sam Carpacci, the woman who married an industrialist, is she?"

I didn't know what she was talking about. "I don't think so."

"Then I'm afraid I've never heard of her."

"It's a pond, Mom. Not a person," Tina said patiently. "Let's not talk about Sam Carpacci, okay?" She pulled a thread from the bottom of her jeans, then said, "Mom, you'll never guess. Tomorrow I'm going to Ally's to learn disco."

That was the first I'd heard of it.

"Marvelous!" Tina's mother said, like she was imitating a movie star. "Then you can teach me and Sam." She did a dance kind of like a waltz. "I'm sure they have a disco orchestra at the Bellagio. I'll have to find my boa." She squinted like she was thinking where it could be.

Sam must have been her boyfriend. I looked at Tina to see if she liked him or not, but I couldn't tell. Tina was chewing on her thumbnail.

No doubt about it, Tina's mother was very strange.

Like she was playacting all the time. "What's a boa?" I asked.

"A boa is a shawl, a long scarf, made of thousands of beautiful feathers."

"Hey, Mom," Tina said. "Could they be pigeon feathers? I'm collecting them."

"Pigeons, my dear, are the rodents of the air. They have a social disease. It's called flocking."

✳

When it was time to go home, Tina's mother said she'd drive me. She led us out to a brand-new red sports car. There was only a small space in the back for me to squeeze into. "Don't you *love* it?" she said. "Every beautiful woman deserves a sports car. You know what they say about old cars."

"No," Tina and I said at the same time.

Then there was silence.

"What, Mom?" Tina said. "What do people say about old cars?"

"I was hoping you knew." She started the car, then pushed a button on the dashboard and the top lifted up and tucked itself in behind me. "Hold on to your hats," she said, and sped out of the 7-Eleven parking lot so fast I thought I'd fly right out of the car.

✳ Chapter Fourteen ✳

At dinner that night I told my mom and dad how I was going to teach my new friend Tina to disco. "Can she come over after school tomorrow?" I asked. "I can show her the *Saturday Night Fever* tape."

"What a good idea," my mother said.

"Disco in the basement," my father said. "I'll think I've died and gone to heaven."

✳

The next day Tina was back in school, but she seemed a little distant. She didn't raise her hand once for Mrs. No Joy to ignore her. And at lunch she hardly touched her food. Then, after school let out, she had to run back to get her jacket because she'd forgotten to put it on. I waited for her, and we hurried to the bus together.

We sat in the front seat again with George. Tina had already told him at lunch how I was going to teach her to disco. Now he said, "I don't think I've ever even seen disco."

I couldn't believe it. "Have *you* seen disco?" it occurred to me to ask Tina.

"Nope." She shook her head and shrugged.

I felt so sorry for them. And then I thanked my Lucky Stars my parents were old, because before I was born they'd been disco maniacs. "You wait," I told Tina. "You're going to flip."

※

Tina and I walked in my front door and dropped our books on the bench in the hall. She followed me into the living room, where my mom was reading a magazine. "Mom," I said, "this is Tina."

My mother took off her glasses and stood up.

Tina walked over and held out her hand to shake.

My mother dropped her magazine to give Tina her hand. "Nice to meet you, Tina." She looked amused. "Come on, I made you girls a snack."

We followed her into the kitchen, where she handed Tina a big bowl of popcorn to carry and me two glasses of juice.

"My mother thinks soda's poison," I explained to Tina. "Like if you take one sip you'll die."

"Let's not exaggerate, Ally." My mother put her hand on my shoulder to kind of steer me out of the kitchen.

"Do you have any extra butter?" Tina asked.

"It's butter flavored," my mother said. "The tape's in the machine, Ally. Try not to make a mess, honey, okay?" I used to wish my mother wasn't such a clean freak, but after visiting Tina's messy house, I was thinking about changing my mind.

Because *Saturday Night Fever* was rated R, my uncle Raymond had made a tape for me of only the opening scene and the dances.

In the basement, Tina sat on the sofa with the bowl of popcorn in her lap, and I placed the glasses of juice on the coffee table. I sat next to her, aimed the remote at the TV, grabbed a handful of popcorn, and we watched the opening. John Travolta walks down a city street to the song "Stayin' Alive," like "Oh boy, I'm cool, look at me," swinging a paint can. Then he sees a pretty girl and grabs his privates like they hurt.

Tina and I played it three times; then the fourth time, we walked around the room like John Travolta. "This is important," I explained, thinking that if Tina could learn, we might actually be able to disco in the talent show. "You have to have attitude." I knew this because my father once explained to me, "Disco's all attitude. You strut your stuff like a cock." *Cock* is another word for rooster, which means you have to stick your chest out.

Tina was pretty good at the disco walk.

We sat back down and watched all the dances; then I played the tape again for the music. I pulled Tina to her feet, wrapped my arm around her back, held her other hand, and started to dance real slow, pushing on her hand so we opened out like butterfly wings do, then came back to holding hands, and out again like butterfly wings.

I twirled her and she started giggling. I kept the disco attitude. I twirled her again, and kept twirling till she stopped giggling and came around to face me on the beat.

"Good," I said. "That's really good. The trick to dancing is always look in your partner's eyes. If you look in my eyes, you'll know when I'm going to make a move." I gave Tina a look, then spun her out and reeled her in.

I explained that with disco it's important to stand straight and formal, kind of like an old-fashioned king and queen at a ball. "Only it's disco," I said. "So it's gritty, too. Like John Travolta swaggering down the street."

"This is so cool!" Tina said. "I never danced like this before. I'm going to teach my grandfather. Let's have a disco party. We'll decorate the basement, hang streamers and balloons. Maybe we can find one of those lights like they have in the movie. We'll invite George and Karl and Lulu and Sissy."

That would never happen, but I didn't tell Tina.

Out of the blue, I heard my father call from up the stairs, "Is there dancing in this house?"

"Yes!" Tina yelled.

"I'm coming down!" Suddenly my father and mother were both racing down the stairs. My father grabbed the remote and forwarded to the Funky Chicken segment.

The Funky Chicken is a line dance where one of the moves is to put your hands in your armpits and flap your elbows like chickens.

"Okay, everybody, line up." My father waved us over. The four of us stood side by side, and the next thing you know, we were all doing the Funky Chicken. Every time we turned in my father's direction, my mother slapped his butt. Every time we turned in my mother's direction, my father slapped hers.

Tina was a quick learner. She had the dance down by the time we finished. "Again!" she said. "Let's do it again."

"Another time," my mother said. My mom can only have a little fun. Too much makes her uncomfortable or something. "It's our dinnertime," she said, herding us up the stairs. "What time's her mother picking her up?" she whispered to me.

Tina heard her. "I'm sure she's just late from work, Mrs. Miller," she answered. "I can walk. I know the way."

"I'm not having a ten-year-old walking the streets at dusk," my father said. "Come on, get in the truck."

I went along for the ride and let Tina sit up front with my dad. "What does your mother do for work?" my father asked her without taking his eyes off the road.

"She paints trompe l'oeil."

"And who hires her?"

"Oh, people. Once she painted a loft in Boston. Sometimes she doesn't get enough work and then she has to do other stuff. Two years ago she was a waitress at Ho Jo's. One time she did telemarketing, selling pet breath fresheners. She had to tell people it made your pet's breath smell like mountain dew, but it just smelled like mint really. She only sold twelve."

When we pulled into the 7-Eleven parking lot we could see that there were no lights on in Tina's house. "You sure you're okay?" my father asked.

"Oh, yes, thank you. I'm fine. Sometimes my mom has to stay till seven. I warm up the oven. We like frozen pizzas."

My father and I waited till Tina walked in the door,

turned on the light, and waved from the window. Then we drove off.

"So, that's your new friend?" my father asked as we pulled onto the road.

"Yes," I said. "She came from Massachusetts. Her grandfather lives on an island."

"She doesn't have a father?"

Tina and I had never spoken about it, but I knew she didn't. "Nope."

"Does her mother leave her alone a lot?"

"I don't know."

"I don't want you over there unless her mother's home, Ally. You understand?"

"Why? We don't do anything bad."

"That doesn't matter."

"Then can she come to our house?"

"You know the rules. Get your mother's permission first."

"I always do."

"Good."

At home the pork chops were on the table. "Dinner's cold," my mother said, motioning for us to hurry up and sit down. She sounded annoyed.

"What was I supposed to do, Janice, make her walk?"

"Didn't anybody teach her manners?" My mother poured milk into my glass. "Did you hear her ask for more butter on her popcorn?"

I would have liked more butter too. "But she's a quick learner," I said. "She can dance disco already. You should dance with her, Mom."

My mother didn't say whether she would or she wouldn't.

"Can Tina come over tomorrow?"

✳ Chapter Fifteen ✳

Tina took the bus home with me again the next day, and we went directly into the basement. I showed her the *Dirty Dancing* DVD. I had an idea.

"*Dirty Dancing!*" Tina grabbed it. "It's my favorite movie *ever.*"

My mother only let me see it this fall. I guess because a girl gets pregnant, and a bunch of teenagers dance dirty, which means you're glued to your partner, with a lot of humping and grinding and girls lifting up their skirts.

Tina and I lay on the sofa, our heads on opposite armrests, our legs intertwined, until the last scene: the last dance. Then I rolled off and kneeled in front of the TV. Tina kneeled next to me.

Johnny Castle, the dance teacher, had taught Baby,

the main character, how to dance at a summer resort. Johnny had been fired for something he didn't do, but then in the last scene he returns in the middle of the gala end-of-summer performance, pulls Baby onto the stage, draws her to him, and reels her out. They're so good nobody can believe their eyes. Johnny jumps off the stage and leads the other dirty dancers, knees bent, fingers snapping, from the audience onto the stage. Even though she'd tried about a million times, Baby had never been able to run and jump high enough for Johnny to lift her over his head. This time she flies into Johnny's arms, in a perfect swan dive.

Watching it, I got goose bumps, and my eyes blurred with tears. It happens every time. Sometimes tears come when you're happy for someone else, especially a character in a movie.

Tina leaned into me on the floor and dropped her head on my shoulder. "Do you ever dance by yourself and make up stories?" she asked.

"Are you kidding? All the time." I'd made one up just a few nights before. "Remember that poem I wrote about the Man in the Moon eating pie?" I asked. "I made up a dance to it. The Man in the Moon tap-dances down to Earth on a moonbeam and knocks on the Lovely Lady's window, and then they dance all around the house."

"They'd fall in love and go to the Moon Ball," Tina said. "He'd wear a tuxedo, and she'd wear a ruby red jeweled dress. The men in the moons from all the other galaxies would be there with their lovely ladies too. . . . Ally! Let's be the Man in the Moon and the Lovely Lady in the talent show. Remember at my house when we danced all jazzy and crazy? We could start out all waltzing and everything and then just go wild."

"Tina," I said, my heart racing, "let's disco. Let's be the Lovely Lady and the Man in the Moon at the *Disco Moon Ball!*"

✳ Chapter Sixteen ✳

Before homeroom on the last day to sign up for the talent show, Tina and I met at Ms. Wiley's door, and together we wrote "Tina Tamblin and Ally Theresa Miller"; then under "category" we wrote "Dance."

At recess later that day, we sat against a tree, and Tina said, "If we win let's use the five hundred dollars for dance lessons—in New York City."

"We could take hip-hop!" I said. We both jumped up and started hip-hopping to no music. Tina looked like a broken Pinocchio with his puppet wires messed up.

Just then, I saw Betsy and Mona walking toward us through the swings and around the sand pit.

Mona tilted her head to one shoulder and said, "One freak." She tilted her head to the other shoulder, and said, "Plus one freak, equals . . ."

She held her palm out, presenting Betsy, who said, "Freak Show."

While they walked away, I felt a pain in my heart, but then Tina said, "Next time let's bend over and fart," which made me laugh.

We lay down on the grass next to the tree and stared at the sky. After we'd been quiet for a moment, I asked her, "Do you believe in Lucky Stars?"

"Like wishing on a star?"

"More like you thank them, because they help you," I said.

"I never thought of that. I bet I do have lucky stars, though. I feel lucky a lot, don't you?"

"Why do you feel lucky? You're not lucky Kirby doesn't write to you," I reminded her.

"But I'm lucky I'm friends with you," she said.

I smiled.

The recess bell rang. I stood up, gave Tina my hand, and pulled her up after me.

$\star$

Before we even placed our trays down on our lunch table, Tina blurted out to George and Karl, "We're going to disco at the Moon Ball." She held her arms out straight in front of her and drew a circle with them in one direction while she circled her hips in the other. "In the talent show!"

"Disco?" Karl burped but not on purpose.

"You ever hear Van Morrison's 'Moondance'?" George asked. He wadded his ice cream wrapper and dropped it in the middle of his spaghetti. "I don't know if you could disco to it. But I have it, if you want."

"I don't think it would work unless it's disco," I said.

"I'll bring it to school so you can listen to it," George said.

"There's no time," I said. It was Friday. The weekend was coming up and we needed to practice. Mrs. No Joy had read an announcement at the start of class. On Tuesday, talent show participants were to spend the second half of the day rehearsing in the auditorium, and Ms. Wiley would decide on the performance lineup. She'd also offer coaching to anyone who needed it.

"You could bring the CD to Ally's on Saturday," Tina suggested. "We'll have to rehearse."

"I'm coming too," Karl said.

"Wait! Who says you can all come to my house?"

"Let's invite Lulu and Sissy and have a real Moon Ball!" said Tina.

"My mother. She won't allow it. I know her."

"She won't care if we're in the yard, will she?" Tina asked.

I hoped Tina was right.

✳ Chapter Seventeen ✳

When I asked my mother if kids could come over to rehearse for the talent show in the yard, she said, "Honey, I don't care. I just hope nobody slips on those leaves." My father had only raked once all fall, so leaves lay in little hills where the wind had blown them.

Now, as I waited for my friends to arrive, the oak's thick, strong limbs reminded me of muscleman arms, and the willow's branches twittered in the wind. Pacing from the oak to the willow and back, I thought about the strange dream I'd had the night before. I was in an old theater inside a golden cage flying in huge arcs over an audience. It wasn't like I was trapped. I could get out of the cage whenever I wanted, but I had to fly and I was afraid I didn't know how to.

I heard Sissy's back door slam at the same moment Tina's mother roared up with the top down. Tina was in front and Lulu was in back, waving before they even rounded the corner into the driveway.

I ran up to the car. "Hi, Mrs. Tamblin," I said.

"Mrs. Tamblin's a fishwife. I'm Mrs. Carpacci," she said, flipping down the visor and stretching her face toward it.

"Mom." Tina climbed out. "That's not your name."

"I'm getting married in the morning," she sang, fluffing her hair out.

"You are not."

"Wait and see."

Tina slammed the door and took Lulu's hand. Her mother tooted goodbye as Sissy walked up.

"Your mommy's getting married?" Lulu asked.

"She's just kidding," Tina said.

It seemed like Tina's mother was odder every time I saw her. I felt sorry for Tina. It would be horrible to have a mother like that.

"This is your house?" Lulu asked me. Her hair was in Princess Leia buns like Tina's, and she still held Tina's hand.

Sissy grabbed mine. It was the first time she ever had.

"Yes, this is my house," I told Lulu. "And this is Sissy, and this is Lulu," I said, introducing them.

"I'm going to disco," Sissy announced.

"Me too," said Lulu, and then they ran their eyes all over each other.

While I opened the garage door and set the boom box on a stool, Tina began teaching the girls the basic disco step. Just then George and Karl rode up on their bikes and laid them on the lawn.

"Come on!" Tina called. "Dance with us."

"Tina!" I stomped both my feet, which I guess is a jump. "This is supposed to be a rehearsal. You guys," I said to Lulu and Sissy, "sit over here." I pointed to the ground next to me, just under the willow branches. "George and Karl, would you please sit down too?"

"We're the audience," Sissy said.

"When we're done, you guys can tell us what you

think, okay? Have you ever seen Fred Astaire and Ginger Rogers?"

They shook their heads.

"*Singin' in the Rain? Dirty Dancing?*"

No again.

"Have you seen MTV?"

"Of course," Karl said.

"Well, we're probably not going to look like that. Just tell us if it doesn't look good."

"Here." Karl dragged a line in the leaves with a stick. "This will be your stage. I'm making it smaller so once you're on the real stage you won't fall off."

"You want 'Moondance'?" George held out the CD.

I'd completely forgotten.

"The first track," George said.

I pointed to the boom box, and he walked over and slipped the CD in, then waited till we were ready.

I held Tina's hand and positioned my right hand on her back. I reminded her to lift her elbow. "Remember. Look in my eyes." I nodded to George and we were off.

The music was a little jazzy, not disco at all. But it worked if you danced twice as fast or twice as slow. We did both. We were like two speeds on a blender. It was kind of cool. We got to the end without too many mistakes. But then when Tina ran and jumped, my feet slipped out from under me and I fell on my butt.

It was hard to tell if our audience cheered because we fell or because they liked our dance.

"We were great!" Tina said in a gush of breath.

"We fell."

"But that's okay. Just like how you're supposed to say 'Break a leg,' instead of 'Good luck' or 'Good show.' It's a superstition."

I didn't understand what on earth she was talking about.

"I want to disco!" Lulu yelled.

"Me too!" Sissy yelled.

"Where'd you learn that, anyway?" Karl asked.

"My parents taught me," I said.

"Cool," said George. "But that song didn't work. Do you have a disco song I can listen to? I need to hear the beat."

"George is going to play it on the violin!" Tina did a cheerleader's jump.

"No, I'm not," George said. "I'm going to find you another song."

"Karl, I bet you can make a black light!" Tina said. "It makes white things look like they glow in the dark."

"I'd have to see one."

"Or you could just stand on a ladder with a fan and blow tiny white pieces of paper onto the stage. They'll look just like whirling stars for the Moon Ball. You think you could?"

"Wait a minute. We're not doing this show with you," Karl reminded her.

I ran into the house and got a Donna Summer CD. Lulu and Sissy did their own disco dance while I added some dazzle to ours. First I taught Tina the Tango Hustle, where you bend way back and step high for three steps, then turn and walk in the opposite direction for three steps. Then I taught her the straight Hustle, which is where you stop, face each other, hold hands and kind of twist your feet and knees back and forth. Then we practiced the jump and fell again.

There was a rustle and a giggle. I looked toward the road and there standing on the sidewalk were Betsy and Mona.

"Oh, no!" I said to Tina.

"They're just jealous," Tina whispered. "What do you think this is, a free show?" she called to them.

"It's a free country," Betsy called back.

"We're not standing in your yard," Mona added.

"Smile, act like you're having fun," I whispered to Tina.

"I don't have to act. I *am* having fun," she said.

"Go home!" Lulu yelled, then ran up to Betsy and Mona, her hands on her hips, and stood there, staring them down.

Sissy ran right behind, jammed her hands on her hips too, and yelled, "Shooo!"

Betsy and Mona glared at them while Tina, George, Karl, and I burst out laughing.

Betsy and Mona tried not to look embarrassed as they slunk away.

✳ Chapter Eighteen ✳

Because it was as warm as spring the next day, Sunday, I called Tina and suggested we pack a picnic and go to Laurel Pond to practice. When she rode up on her bike, I got my bike out of the garage and placed the boom box in my bike basket. Tina put our lunches in hers, and we hopped on our bikes and sped off.

A few blocks from the path through the woods that leads to the pond, we ran into a yard sale I couldn't pass up. Well, to tell you the truth, I've never run into a yard sale I could pass up. It used to drive Betsy nuts.

Tina only had two dollars or I swear she would have bought about ten things, including an emerald-speckled bowling ball.

At the free bin next to the cash box, I picked up a cool card of a gorilla holding a bouquet of glitter roses. I showed it to Tina, because I thought it probably looked like her stuffed monkey Philip, and she said we should buy it and keep it for a good-luck charm. I opened it up and read out loud, "To Philomena, Keep your double chin up. Love, Freddy."

We'd left our bikes at the end of the driveway by the mailbox. After we got back to them, I dropped the card in my basket, kicked my kickstand, and noticed the name on the mailbox. You'll never guess what it was.

"Miller!" I shouted. "This card is probably from Freddy Miller to his relative Philomena Miller!" I dropped it to the ground like it was covered with scorpions. "What if it's a bad omen?"

"Why would it be?" Tina asked.

"Remember when Ms. Creeley asked me if I was related to Freddy Miller? He's like a juvenile delinquent. That's why Mrs. No Joy put me in the seat right in front of her. I never want to see Freddy Miller's face as long as I live. And now I've touched his signature. Ooooooooh!" I shook my fingers to decontaminate them.

"Let's throw it in the pond," Tina suggested.

That seemed like an excellent idea.

Tina dropped it in her basket; then, as we pedaled, she said, "Hey, where's the town dump? I still haven't found it."

"It's far. Why?"

"I was thinking I might find Philip there."

"You threw him away?"

"My mother got rid of our old car with him in it."

"Weren't you mad?" I asked.

"Yes. But not really. I mean, there's nothing I can do. It's kind of complicated. Sometimes my mother doesn't think about those sorts of things."

Wasn't not thinking about your daughter's stuffed monkey called being inconsiderate—or mean? "I'd be mad," I said.

I really wanted to ask her why her mother did such weird things, but Tina pedaled away from me like she was running away from the subject.

Once I caught up with her, we were already at the path into the woods. We hopped off our bikes and Tina followed me as we steered down the narrow path covered with leaves. We walked a long way, hearing only the sounds of our bike tires rolling and the snapping of twigs. When we saw the pond, Tina gasped and covered her mouth with her hand. "It's so beautiful," she said.

The trees were reflected in its surface, which was smooth as glass. "And so quiet," I said.

We laid our bikes on the grass. Tina handed me my lunch; then we sat on a rock by the water. I took out my juice box, a plastic bag with four Fig Newtons inside, and my egg salad sandwich. All Tina had was Twinkies and chocolate milk.

"Didn't you bring a sandwich?" I asked her.

"I got these at the Seven-Eleven."

My mother had packed my lunch for me. Tina's mother had probably never packed a lunch for Tina in her whole life.

I gave Tina half of my sandwich and traded two Fig Newtons for a Twinkie.

"Remember the first day of school we were wearing the same leggings?" I asked her.

"I love those pants. They're too short, but I still wear them."

"Those were the pants Betsy and I were going to wear on the first day to be like twins. I started crying because she didn't wear them. Well, really because she'd dumped me for Mona. It was awful."

"I never cry."

"Really? *Never?*"

"Not since I was little."

"If I had to choose between never crying and crying all the time, I'd choose never," I said.

"But sometimes things are sad. My mother had to go to a hospital and stay for four months once." Tina hugged her knees.

"What was the matter with her?"

"A disease." She crumpled up her Twinkie wrapper.

"What disease?"

She looked around for a trash can so she could get up and leave the conversation, but of course there was none. So she went back to hugging her knees.

"What disease?" I asked again.

"It's called bipolar. I went to stay with my grandfather. That was okay. I mean, it was great on Rock Island, but I was afraid my mother wouldn't get better. Still, I never cried."

"Is she okay now?"

"Only if she takes her medication . . . Hey." Tina stood up suddenly. "Let's rehearse."

I wanted to ask her more, but Tina was already at the bikes lifting out the boom box.

We pretended the pond was our audience. "This is our new ending," I told Tina. I put her hand on my shoulder and instructed, "Follow my lead." I strutted like a proud cock, my chest puffed out, my chin tucked in. "We walk off the stage like this."

"After the jump," Tina said.

"The jump doesn't work," I said. "We don't have enough time to figure it out. And anyway, I don't think I'm strong enough."

"Sure you are. If Baby and Johnny could do it, so can we. We just have to practice more."

"That's a movie. There's not enough time," I insisted. "Come on, let's start from the beginning." I put on Gloria Gaynor's "I Will Survive," and we ran through our dance another time. Tina kept trying to jazz it up by waving her arms in huge arcs and swaying her hips too much. So I reminded her again that disco is formal. Disco is attitude. Disco is stiff.

Tina nodded as though she agreed.

"Hey, the card!" she shouted. She got it out of her bike basket and brought it over to the pond. Holding it up so we could look at the grinning gorilla, she said, "Bye, Freddy Miller." Then she tossed it into the water.

"Good riddance, Freddy Miller," I said.

The gorilla floated in the water at our feet, smiling at us. Kind of sadly.

Tina got quiet. "Are you thinking of Philip?" I asked her.

She nodded.

"Was he your favorite stuffed animal?"

She nodded again.

"I have a doll named Katie, after my dead sister."

"You had a sister? She died?"

"Before I was born. I never knew her. But I think I'd cry if my mother left my doll in a car she brought to the dump."

"I know."

"Do you want to keep the card?" The top of it hadn't even gotten wet yet. "I mean, Freddy Miller isn't bad luck for *you*. It'll be kind of like having Philip again."

"Thanks," she said, bending down to lift the card out of the water.

✴

The night before the run-through, I lay in my bed looking out the window at the sky. There was no moon but there were a zillion stars, layers and layers of them, some bright and twinkling and some so far away they were a white smudge. They made me think about God. My grandmother goes to church every Sunday, and when I visit her in Chicago, I go with her. She told me that heaven isn't up in the sky. Heaven is in your heart.

She said that God is everywhere, even inside of you. "God," she said, "is love. Pure love. And if you let the sweetness and love shine inside you, then when you die you'll have sweetness and love all around you, all the time, everywhere."

I told her that I never have sweetness and love inside of me. And she said, "Nonsense, of course you do, but you also have anger and fear, jealousy, even hate sometimes — and lots more. That's what it means to be human. It's hard to do, but when you have hurtful feelings, try to send them away, just float them into the sky like balloons."

Tomorrow, I would sit in the auditorium and watch Betsy and her band being too cool. I knew I'd feel jealous and filled with hate for Mona. I made a plan to breathe deeply and imagine my breath, stinking of those bad feelings, filling up a huge blimp that would get picked up by a breeze and travel all the way across the Atlantic Ocean to Europe, where it would start leaking out stinky air. All the people in a small mountain village in Switzerland would look up at the blimp and hold their noses.

What if Tina and I stunk? What if I froze when it was time for Tina and me to perform?

I picked out the brightest star in the sky and decided it was my lucky one. *Please*, I begged. *Let me and Tina shine.*

✶ Chapter Nineteen ✶

At the run-through, Tina swiveled in her seat, looking around while everyone waited for Ms. Wiley to begin. Kids had spread out all over the auditorium. Some were dropping their butts on the folded seats, slamming them down. A few were singing, rehearsing their acts. Artie and Stu did Tae Kwon Do in the aisle next to us.

"Where are they?" Tina asked me.

"Who?" I asked her.

"Karl and George."

I couldn't believe her. On Saturday as they were about to leave, Tina had stood in front of their bikes, grabbed their handlebars, and said, "You can't go until you promise to be in the show."

They'd looked at each other, shrugged, and said, "Promise."

But as they rode off, Karl had yelled, "Sucker!"

How could Tina not remember? "Tina," I said. "They're not in the show."

"I'm going to ask Ms. Wiley for a pass to go get them." Tina stood up.

"She won't give you one," I began to say, but Tina was halfway down the aisle to the stage.

Artie and Stu plopped down behind me, then bumped the back of my seat with their feet.

"Cut it out!" I snapped.

"Cut it out!" Artie imitated me in a girly voice and bumped again. "Everybody's going to boo you," he sang in my ear.

I ignored him and moved to a seat on the other side of the aisle.

Tina got right beneath the stage and just stood there, until finally Ms. Wiley bent down to listen. I could see Betsy and her band eavesdropping from the front row. Betsy turned to look around the auditorium until she saw me. Our eyes met and she half smiled before turning back around.

My heart skipped a beat. What had made her do that? I wondered.

When Tina came back, she told me that Ms. Wiley said there wasn't enough time to go get anyone. "I bet they're sick," she said.

"They're not sick. I saw George on the bus. They don't want to be in our act. They said it a thousand times."

"They'd have so much fun. We still have two weeks. They'll change their minds."

Suddenly I had a horrible thought. What if Tina wasn't seeing things the way they really were? What if she was wacky like her mother? Was I out of my mind to be dancing disco with her?

From the stage, Ms. Wiley started to explain that she'd be taking us more or less randomly. Once she saw our acts, she'd decide what order to place us in.

"Now I need you to be quiet and polite while others are performing. When I call your name, please step directly to the stage. I have asked you to keep your acts short. We don't have a hook, but I will stop you at five minutes on the dot. We have a lot to get through today. It would be very nice if we could get home in time for dinner tonight."

In the first act, two boys from one of the other fifth-grade classes wrestled. One was twice the size of the other, and the big one held the little one over his head like he was King Kong.

Two girls from another class lip-synched to the song from *Moulin Rouge* with pretend microphones that they tossed from one hand to the other, swinging their hips. They didn't catch the microphones at the same time or in the same hands, and their hips couldn't keep the beat.

The next kids, two boys and two girls, did a skit about Martians invading the White House.

"Louder," Ms. Wiley said. "We need to hear you in the back row. Pretend you're talking to a person all the way back there."

So they shouted.

My hands started to sweat and freeze at the same time. I jiggled my foot, then my hips, then my shoulders. I couldn't stop them. There were jumping beans inside me. I jumped up and kind of shimmied against the side wall to the back of the auditorium.

Tina followed me.

"I can't," I said.

"You just have stage fright. Don't worry."

"What if they laugh at us? What if they boo?"

"They're going to cheer."

Ms. Creeley entered the auditorium and stood in front of the stage with Ms. Wiley. "Is Tina Tamblin here?" she called.

"Here!" Tina waved.

"I need you in the office."

We wouldn't have to dance after all!

Tina ran down the aisle.

"Please walk," Ms. Wiley called to her.

Ms. Creeley said something to Ms. Wiley, then Ms. Wiley called, "Ally? We have enough time to see your and Tina's act."

My stomach felt like somebody had just kicked it.

Ms. Wiley squinted out over the audience "Ally? Are you here?"

I wished I could faint and wake up in two weeks. I began to walk to my execution. Ms. Creeley smiled and winked at me.

Tina took my hand. I placed my other hand in the middle of her back and waited for "I Will Survive" to begin.

We stood there—Forever.

"Music?" Ms. Wiley finally said, which made the kids in the audience laugh. "All right, everybody. Simmer down."

I remembered. "It's in my backpack," I whispered to Tina, who ran to get it, then came right back. When Ms. Wiley turned the CD player on, I could feel my chest shiver. As the music began, I shouted under my breath, "Don't. Don't. Don't," telling myself not to cry.

I tried to open Tina out like a wing, but she wouldn't budge.

"What's the matter?" I whispered.

"You said, 'Don't.' "

"Go!" I twirled her, trying to catch up to the music by

skipping a couple of steps, which confused Tina. I forgot to look in her eyes. When I pushed her shoulder to spin her out, I did it too hard. We let go of each other's hands and she almost fell. We came together. I tried pushing her out again, her in one direction, me in the other. But I spun one and a half times and ended up facing the back wall. So Tina slapped my behind, and the audience roared. We twisted our knees and feet for half a minute, frozen. I'd forgotten what else to do.

In the front row, I saw Mona giggling, while Betsy held her hand over her mouth, her eyes huge, like she couldn't believe what she was seeing.

"Jump!" Tina whispered, and started skipping backward, making big arcs with her arms.

We weren't supposed to jump!

Tina ran at me, jumped, and knocked me backward into a somersault.

She landed on top of me.

Everybody laughed, including Tina. "It's funny," she whispered in my ear, then sat up and rode me like a horsy.

I turned my hips to slide her off, then ran from the stage. There was no way out. I hid behind the curtain, trapped.

By the time Tina reached me, I was crying.

"Ally, don't."

"We were horrible!"

"It wasn't horrible. It was funny."

I shook my head.

And before I could escape, Ms. Creeley appeared out of nowhere.

She walked right up to me, saw my tearstained face, and pulled me to her chest. I was afraid my tears would stain her blouse and tried to pull away, but she wouldn't let me. She patted my back. Tina patted it too. Ms. Creeley led us to a door behind a curtain at the back of the stage, and we stepped into the hall.

"I don't want to do it anymore," I mumbled to my feet.

"It's okay, Ally, truly it is. You have two whole weeks to work out the kinks. I really don't think you want to be a quitter, do you?" she said, handing me a tissue.

I stared at my feet and shrugged.

"We just need to rehearse more," Tina said.

"Don't lose heart, my dear," Ms. Creeley said, and took Tina off to the office.

"Ally!" Tina called from down the hall. "We forgot to say 'Break a leg!' "

✳ Chapter Twenty ✳

I didn't want to show my face at Heady Hollow Elementary School ever again. It was my fault I freaked out and screwed up the beginning of our dance, but then Tina had turned it into a cartoon, slapping me on the butt, riding me like a horse. Every idea she had, she turned into a really stupid comedy. Rabbits out of hats that are rats. George wiggling his ears while he played the violin. I should have known better than to think she could actually dance proper disco, with dignity, stiffness, and attitude.

I never wanted to speak to Tina again.

The next morning, I faked a sore throat. Usually, my mother would make me drink a gallon of orange juice, take Tylenol, and stay in bed or on the couch all day, which is like a mini-vacation, considering I am allowed to watch nonstop TV.

But I'd been so upset when I came home from the run-through that I'd blurted out everything.

So instead of handing me a glass of orange juice and some Tylenol, she whipped out a thermometer. Of course, my temperature was normal. She told me I probably had an emotional hangover from yesterday and it was better to face my embarrassment sooner than later.

I begged for a ride to school and my father drove me. "Buck up, Buckaroo," he said, patting my head.

I wanted to say, "Shut up, Liver for Dinner," and smack him.

I climbed out of the car with a big gray cloud over my head. I stared straight ahead so I wouldn't have to look at anyone as I walked to my classroom. I dreaded seeing Tina and Betsy and Mona, every single kid who'd been in that auditorium, Ms. Wiley, and especially Ms. Cree-ley, because she'd certainly try to convince me to dance again.

Thank you, Lucky Stars, the buses hadn't arrived yet. The halls were almost empty and so was my classroom. I sat down and stared at a long scratch in my desk. It seemed familiar, like it had always been there, but I was sure I'd never noticed it before.

Tina walked in just as class was about to begin. She sat down, then tapped my elbow to hand me a note. It said, "Let's rehearse every day." Underneath, she'd drawn one beaver slapping another beaver on the butt. I hid my hands under the desk and tore it into tiny pieces.

Meanwhile, for the first time ever, Mrs. No Joy beamed in front of the class. "I'm sure those of you in the talent show will be pleased to hear that I've been asked to be a judge," she began. "Not many people know that in my former life I was a concert pianist. I thought I'd be touring Europe until well into my middle years, but premature arthritis set in. And so I teach. Don't ever count your chickens before they're hatched, people. Now, just because I'm your teacher, it does not mean that you're at any advantage whatsoever. I will not be partial in any way. If you deserve to win, you'll win, and if you don't, you won't. Simple as that."

Harry Crick, who was going to walk on stilts, raised his hand and asked Mrs. No Joy if she was going to be the only judge.

"Did I say I was the only judge? That, people, is how rumors get started."

Some more kids raised their hands, including Betsy.

"If you have questions, ask Ms. Wiley. Now take out your science books."

I could hardly wait to hear how Tina would turn Mrs. No Joy's being a judge into a good thing. Because she would. She turned everything around, all the time, every minute.

When I passed Betsy's table at lunch, she smiled at me again. I smiled back and sneaked a look at the rest of her table. I was afraid to *really* look, so they were kind of a blur, but I could swear they were all smiling at me. Even the dreaded Mona.

I worried that they had some terrible torture up their sleeves.

Tina was still in the classroom with Mrs. No Joy because of a problem with her homework. We'd been given two weeks to write a report on any state but New Jersey. She'd chosen Florida and written twelve pages when it was supposed to be only two. Mrs. No Joy was probably telling her to do it over again and follow directions this time.

At our table Karl said, "Well?" and George said, "How'd it go?" They were asking about the run-through, of course.

"On a scale of one to ten," I told them, "I'd say zero." I stared at my fish sticks.

"What happened?" Karl and George asked together.

"Remember how we fell on the lawn that day you came over? I told Tina we weren't doing the jump, but of course she jumps anyway. Boom! On my butt. Then she rode me like a horse!"

"She didn't!" Karl's eyes were bugging, and I could tell he was holding himself back from laughing.

"Wow." George stared at me hard. "And everybody laughed."

"Exactly. So I quit. I'm not doing it again. Tina doesn't know. Even when I tell her I quit she won't believe me. Watch. When she comes in, ask her how it went. I bet you a million dollars she says, 'Great!' "

"Eternal optimist," Karl replied.

Just then Tina showed up.

"Where were you guys?" she asked George and Karl.

"When?" They had no idea what she was talking about.

"You didn't come to the run-through."

"Tina!" I practically screamed. "They don't want to be in the show. *I* don't want to be in the show."

"But we were great. The audience loved us."

"Because they laughed? They laughed because we were ridiculous."

"But you can't quit," she insisted. "You heard what Ms. Creeley said. All we need is more practice. We have two whole weeks."

I looked deep into her eyes to make sure she'd hear me. "I already made up my mind. I don't want to talk about it anymore."

Tina stared off in the distance. "But you'll do magic?" she finally asked.

I had to be absolutely clear or she'd turn whatever I said around to mean "Yes."

"No. I won't," I said.

"It just takes not being afraid."

"It takes not turning every single thing into a joke." I took a sip through my straw.

Tina went back to staring. She'd finally stopped talking, and it was a little scary.

"You can do magic," George reminded her after a while.

Tina still stared at nothing, so I added, "I'm sorry, Tina. I just can't."

Tina switched her gaze to her fish sticks. After a moment, she picked one up and pointed it at George. "If I do magic," she said, "you'll play sound effects? You won't have to stand on the stage."

George shrugged. "Yeah. Sure."

"Karl, can you make a purple light? Purple's the color for wizards and magicians."

"I think they have gels. I'll talk to Mr. Martinez. I'm pretty sure he does the lights."

"You won't be in the show at all?" Tina asked, turning to me. She sounded genuinely sorry for me, which made it hard to stay mad at her.

I shrugged.

"Ms. Creeley doesn't know you quit?" George asked me.

"Not really. Why?"

"Nothing. It's just that she said something to my mother," he went on.

"What?"

"That your being in the show was her greatest accomplishment so far this year."

"Oh, no," I moaned.

"Come on, Ally, *please*?" Tina begged. "We have two whole weeks. We'll rehearse every day. I'll dance all stiff and formal. I'll have attitude." She puffed out her chest. "I promise."

I shook my head. I didn't want to talk about it anymore.

I changed the subject from me to her. "Why'd Ms. Creeley pull you away yesterday?" I asked.

"Oh. No reason."

"What?"

"It was nothing. Never mind." She wiped her hands on her napkin.

✗

Back home I sat on the sofa in the living room, thinking how weird my only friend was. It made me feel kind of lost. I wondered if it had been a mistake to ever be friends with Tina. It had certainly been a mistake to think she could seriously disco. It was probably impossible for her ever to be stiff and formal for very long. Or to just plain follow rules. Who on earth writes a twelve-page essay when it's supposed to be two? It was like she was just too big. Not physically—she was actually pretty short. It was her whole personality. She couldn't hold herself back. Like raising her hand to answer every single question, even though Mrs. No Joy called on her maybe once a week. But it wasn't like there was some other girl waiting in line to be my friend.

I lifted my legs up onto the sofa back and hung my head off the seat so the whole room appeared upside down. For some reason I had an urge to write a poem, and in a flash I had the first two lines:

> Sometimes buds bloom into big beautiful
>   flowers,
> And sometimes they get eaten by bugs.

I didn't know if the poem, once I finished it, would be about my friendship with Tina or about the talent show. Since kindergarten I'd thought the show would be the highlight of elementary school, but now that dream was all chewed up.

As I stood to go finish the poem in my room, I happened to glance out the picture window and see Betsy walking up the hill, alone.

I quick slipped on my shoes, squeezed through the front door, and sat on the stoop.

Instead of pretending she didn't see me, she smiled at me for the third time in two days. "Too bad about yesterday," she called over.

"It was awful," I blurted out, and then was so surprised we'd spoken to each other, I was tongue-tied.

"Can I come in your yard?" Betsy asked.

I shrugged.

As she walked toward me, my heart skipped. I knew I shouldn't, but I wanted to be her friend as much as ever. To me, Betsy felt like stepping in the front door after a long, long time away from home.

"Ally Star?" she said when she reached me. That was her nickname for me because I was always thanking my Lucky Stars. "I heard you quit." She sat down next to me.

I nodded.

"I'm glad."

I wondered why, but I just nodded again.

"I know you must be mad at me. And I know this probably is weird. But the girls in the band and I have been talking. We think you should be our go-go dancer. Be part of Ruby."

"What?"

"I'm serious. Actually, it was my mother's and Mona's idea."

"*Mona's* idea?"

"No. Her *mother's*. Ruby's going to win. You didn't see us, but we kicked butt. Ally, you know all those old dances. I forget their names."

She was thinking of dances like the Pony, the Jerk, the Mashed Potato, the Twist, the Monkey, the Hitchhike, the Stroll.

"But you're going to win anyway," I said. "Why do you need me?"

"The truth?"

I wanted to say, "What else is there? A lie?" But I just nodded.

"Mona's mother is in the East Meadow Playhouse. She knows about this kind of stuff. When my mother told her what a good dancer you are, they both thought you should go-go dance with us. I mean, we'll definitely win the talent show. But then there's the state competition. With you, we'd be more unique, you know?"

"What about Mona?"

"What about her?"

"She hates me."

"You hate *her*."

It was true I'd been mean to Mona, but she'd been a million times worse. "You dropped me like a hot potato," I said. "That was so mean when you showed up at the bus stop like that."

"But you never wanted to be friends with anybody else. After Mona and I were at the beach together, I wanted to be her friend and stay friends with you, too. I knew you'd never let me."

"You didn't use to want to be Mona's friend either."

"I changed my mind."

"You didn't have to show up at the bus stop dressed like twins."

"I know. That was bad. I'm sorry."

"It was Mona's idea?" I asked.

"You never wore the leggings again." She hadn't answered my question. "Me neither," she went on. "We should wear them sometime. But no butterfly jersey. It's kind of babyish, don't you think?"

I hadn't thought that, but I believed her if she said so.

"Come on, Ally Star. Please. Be in Ruby with us. It'll be *so* chill."

Chill was a word my cousin Francesca had used. It was a teenage word I'd never heard Betsy use before. It made me feel outdated. "I have to think," I told her.

"You really should dance with us. We'll *win*." She stood up. "Think about it, and call me in an hour, okay?"

I nodded.

After she walked away, I rested my chin in my hands and remembered how go-go dancing with Ruby had been my idea a long time ago. I thought how I should probably thank my Lucky Stars that I'd been invited. I was sure Betsy was right: we'd win the talent show, and maybe the state competition too.

It also meant I'd probably be friends with Charlie and Gracie, and of course, Mona. And even if I couldn't stop hating Mona, maybe I could mostly ignore her.

Still, I couldn't ignore the feeling in my belly that it would be wrong to join Ruby. I stood up and went into the house and got a bag of tortilla chips from the kitchen, then snuck them into my room. I'm not allowed to eat in there. I sat at my desk, crossed my legs, and pumped my foot while I ate one chip after another, thinking how Betsy and Mona had tortured me all year. And now because they needed me, they'd suddenly decided to be nice.

It would feel so satisfying to call Betsy up and say, "Sorry."

Plus, what about Tina? If I agreed to dance with Ruby, wouldn't I be acting toward her the same way Betsy had acted toward me on the first day of school?

But Tina had ridden me like a horse. And the first time I'd ever really spoken to her, she'd run around the hall putting a fire out on her head. Who wore Princess Leia hair, anyway? And who in the whole world rode the school bus to go on a sightseeing tour? Only Tina.

Did I really even want to stay friends with such a goofy person?

Besides, being in Betsy's band was the only way I'd

ever be in the talent show, and hadn't Ms. Creeley told George's mother that my agreeing to be in the show had been her greatest accomplishment this year?

Just thinking about all those old dances made me feel like standing on the bed and doing the Pony. A go-go dancer felt like what I was born to be.

How *could* I say no?

It had been almost an hour since Betsy had left. I sat up and dialed her number for the first time in forever.

"Hello?" she answered.

"Yes!" I shouted.

"Yes!" she shouted back.

✳ Chapter Twenty-one ✳

Betsy had told me on the phone that she'd call the other Rubies and let them know I'd joined the band. She said we'd have rehearsal the next day at Charlie's. After school, she and Mona would pick me up.

Betsy always came in the back way, so I was waiting in the kitchen after school when I heard her and Mona giggling as they walked up to the door. I'd planned to dart out before they had a chance to knock, to avoid the big fuss my mom was sure to make. But my concerned parent walked in just as I was turning the doorknob to leave. "Where're you going?" she asked at the same second Betsy and Mona knocked. "Who's that?"

I opened the door.

"HI!" Betsy and Mona said like a blast of wind.

"Betsy!" My mother beamed. "And Mona, is it? Come in. Come in. To what do we owe this surprise?"

I moved out of their way.

"Ally's joining our band," Mona said, looking around the kitchen. It was the first time she'd ever been in my house.

"We're going to rehearse at Charlie Mordarski's," I added.

"You're not dancing with Tina?" my mother asked.

I'd dreaded that question.

"I *told* you what happened at rehearsal, Mom."

"So you quit?"

"I'm going to go-go dance in Betsy's band and Tina's doing a magic act. It's okay, Mom. Now can we go?" I headed for the door.

"You're going to *go-go* dance?" My mother looked like I'd just been named Coolest Daughter in the Milky Way.

"I know," Betsy said, following me out. "It's so chill."

"Bye, Mrs. Miller," Mona said to my mother, holding up her hand and dipping her knees cutely.

"Bye, girls." My mom stood at the door watching us go single file down our sidewalk.

On the street, it felt *so* creepy that my sworn enemy had invaded my house, and that now she was walking right next to me. Mona and Betsy took really long strides, and to keep up, I had to take huge steps too. I wondered if they'd seen girls walk like that in some movie, like *Charlie's Angels*.

"Remember that day we saw you dancing on your lawn?" Mona said. "We were like, wow!" Her smile reminded me of someone who'd just bit into a horribly bitter lemon but wants you to believe it's as sweet as candy. "We're all really excited."

I felt like saying, "Then how come you called me a freak?"

"Wait till you see Charlie's house," Betsy said. "She has horses."

"But really you need lessons to ride them. I might take some," Mona said, pumping her arms to match her long strides and picking up the pace.

The front lawns in Charlie's neighborhood were smooth as golf courses. Windows sparkled at the street, and not one driveway had a single crack or loose pebble or newspaper somebody forgot to pick up. Charlie's driveway ran up a hill and looped around to the back of the house. It was as long as my whole road. In the back there were a stable and a ring with sawhorses where Charlie jumped her horse.

"That's Charlie's horse." Betsy pointed to a chestnut stallion eating grass up on a hill. Three other horses were near the gate down below.

"He's named Hurricane," Mona said.

" 'Cause he's so wild," Betsy explained. "Nobody can ride him but Charlie."

"But we can ride the others once we have lessons," said Mona.

The swimming pool was in a glass room connected to the rest of the house by a glass hallway lined with plants. Betsy said that the pool room had a skylight in the ceiling that opened in the summertime like a garage door.

Betsy knocked at the back door and Charlie opened it wearing patched jeans. Her purple streak was woven into one long braid down her back. "Hey, all right, *Ally,*" she said, then turned and started walking like we were supposed to follow her, which we did. Betsy walked side by side with Mona, and I followed behind.

Betsy asked Charlie to take us to the pool room so I could see the ceiling open. We walked through the kitchen and the library and down the glass hall to the pool room. Charlie pushed a button on the wall and the ceiling whined open. Some leaves flew in, and then a bird flew in too.

Charlie pushed a button on the intercom and called Javier, their handyman, to catch the bird, but we didn't stay to watch.

We walked through the creaky, dark part of the house, which was built in George Washington's time. The ceilings were low and the windows were small. But in the new wing, the windows were taller than people.

Upstairs, you felt like you were in the trees. Charlie's room was as big as my whole attic. On one side was a four-poster bed and on the other, microphones, speakers, a guitar, drums, and a keyboard stood ready to be played.

I kept waiting for Betsy to look at me so I could make a "Wow!" face, but Gracie walked in and everybody made a fuss about her newly pierced ears. Anyway, Betsy was probably so at home in this mansion, with these girls, that she was beyond "Wow." In addition to the studs Gracie already had in her earlobes, she now had two new studs in her left ear, higher up. Everyone gathered around complimenting her, asking where she'd had it done and if it had hurt.

I just kind of hung back, because I didn't really know Gracie well enough to say anything.

"Gracie," Betsy finally said. "Look who's here!"

I was pretty sure Gracie had already seen me, but now she looked at me and said, "Ally. Cool!"

"So, are we going to play?" Mona said suddenly. "Ally, why don't you sit down and watch us first."

I sat in a chair, and Betsy gave me a thumbs-up as she picked up her guitar and everyone took their positions.

Charlie counted, "A one and a two and a three," and they broke into this great oldie called "Respect." Mona sang the lead, holding the mike with two hands, one foot in front of the other, shifting her weight forward and back. Everyone else sang backup. In the middle of the song, Gracie switched from keyboard to clarinet. It was pretty cool.

"So?" Betsy said when they'd finished. "What do you think?"

If there were a junior *American Idol* show, they'd at least make the finals. "Totally great," I said. "You rock."

"Want to dance while we play it again?" Charlie asked.

I felt shy. "Maybe you should play it one more time."

They played again, and the music was so rocking, I kind of started to do the Hitchhike in my seat, first with only my head, then my shoulders. Then I stuck out my thumb. When I started the Jerk, I had to stand up. I switched to a Mashed Potato strut, where I stuck my chin in and out as my feet did a mini-Charleston. The drums drove me mad and I wanted to heebie-jeebie, but I controlled myself.

"Awesome!" they all said when the song had ended.

"Where do you think you should stand?" Mona asked. "We're like a music video. I can't wait till we win and have a real video. You should see our costumes. Really girly."

"My mother's seamstress is making them," Charlie said. "I mean, you *are* in, right?"

I knew I'd already said yes to Betsy, but for some reason I was too shy to say it again. So I just stood there like I'd swallowed my tongue.

"Come on, Ally, dance next to me," Betsy coaxed. "She's already agreed she's going to dance with us. Right, Ally?"

I walked over to stand by Betsy. She held her hand up for slapping.

"Right." I slapped.

Here's the truth: I never would have been friends with Tina if I could have been friends with Betsy.

But then, thinking about it in the basement that night, I remembered how Tina had called me the day before the disastrous run-through.

"Are you looking out your window?" she'd asked me.

"Now I am," I'd said, getting up to look.

"Do you ever look at the trees in your yard and think about all they've seen?"

The moon was so low in the sky and the big oak was so tall, the moon looked like an ornament in its branches. "Yes," I said. "Do you?"

"Did you ever notice the oak tree in the middle of the Seven-Eleven parking lot?"

I hadn't really, but I said, "Yes," thinking I'd notice it the next time I was at Tina's.

"I bet it came from the same mother tree as the one in your yard. Sometimes I talk to it," Tina said.

I talked to my tree too, but I'd never dreamed I'd ever tell anyone. "Do you ask it what it's seen?" I asked her.

"It says that 2,342 birds were born in its branches. It likes bats. When the wind blows, it tickles and makes the tree laugh. And once an owl lived in it for forty years. What does yours say?"

"Mine says it hates cars and remembers when there weren't even any houses. It told me that a little Indian girl used to sit under it for shade when it was still a sapling. When the girl grew up, she fell in love with a boy from another tribe and they met under the tree. Their parents wouldn't let them marry and the girl used to come alone and cry. Then one day the girl and the boy climbed up a mountain, held hands, and jumped off Suicide Leap."

"There's a suicide leap here?"

"Probably," I said.

"That's so sad," Tina said. "My tree saw George Washington and his troops marching by."

"Mine too!" I'd really thought that.

That day, I'd been so happy that there was another girl in the world who talked to trees and that she was my friend. But it was probably time to stop doing silly things like asking a tree a question and imagining what it answered. Next year I'd be in middle school already. I had to grow up.

I walked upstairs and punched Betsy's number, thanking my Lucky Stars I wasn't calling just to hear her voice.

"Hey," she said. "What's up?"

"I'm glad we're friends."

"I know," she said. "I was just going to call you. Remember how you used to do that swimming dance where you hold your nose like you're going under water?"

"The Swim."

"You should do that one too."

✳

At the bus stop Monday morning, Mona and Betsy practically ran me over. "Ally!" Mona said. "You'll never guess! Oh, my God!"

"Her mother's in community theater—" Betsy started.

"Let me tell." Mona stomped.

Betsy took a step back and crossed her arms.

172

"My mother's in community theater," Mona re-peated. "And a few years ago they had this cage built for one of their productions. So last night at dinner she said, 'Too bad somebody doesn't use that cage in the talent show.' That's when I got the idea."

"You can dance in it!" Betsy piped in.

"My mother said they can hang it from the ceiling above the band. In the sixties they used to go-go dance in them all the time. She even called Ms. Wiley. You can dance in it. Isn't that cool?"

It reminded me of the swinging-cage dream I'd had, flying over the audience. "But won't everyone laugh?"

"Ha ha ha ha ha ha!" Artie Kaminsky must have heard me. He dove to our side of the tree rolling on the ground, holding his stomach, fake-laughing like a maniac.

"Drop dead, infant," Mona said.

Artie laughed more softly.

"Go on." Mona stared at him like her eyes shot bullets.

Artie said, "Ha ha ha," a few times under his breath before slinking back to the other side of the tree.

"They won't laugh," Betsy said. "They'll go like—" She opened her mouth and stared up at the sky like she was seeing God himself floating down.

"Ms. Wiley wanted to know if they could keep the cage at the school for other shows," Mona said. "I can't believe we have a Go-Go Cage. No way we won't win. No way. What size shoes do you wear?"

"Five."

"That's my size. I have white patent leather boots you could borrow."

"She doesn't have to wear those," said Betsy.

"Only if you want to," Mona said. "They were my second cousin's. They're authentic. Like from 1969."

"Authentic." Betsy imitated her. "That just means they're old."

"You're just jealous," Mona said.

"Right. Go-go boots are white and shiny and ugly. Nobody likes them but you."

"Oh, I almost forgot," Mona said to me. "Betsy knows what everybody likes."

"Oh, I almost forgot," Betsy said to me. "Mona knows everything."

"Just call her Encyclopedia." Artie stood in front of Mona and pretended to read her.

Then the bus arrived and ruined all the fun.

Chapter Twenty-two

"**W**ant to come over after school and see my magic act?" Tina asked me the next day. "Wait till you see what I'm doing with my mother's embroidered silk coat."

We were on our way to the cafeteria. I was going to break the news to her about being in Ruby during lunch. I thought that George and Karl's being there would help.

But as we passed by Betsy's table with our trays, Betsy called to me, "You're sitting with us, right? We've got a surprise."

Tina looked from Betsy to me.

"Um . . ." I hesitated.

"Here." Charlie kicked an empty chair to open it out.

"You're friends?" Tina said. "That's good. My grandfather always says forgive and forget."

I set my tray down and sat.

Tina set her tray down next to mine to take the other empty seat.

"Sorry," Mona said. "It's taken."

Tina looked at me.

"I'll tell you about it later," I said.

"Oh, okay," she said.

I watched Tina walk over to George and Karl, thinking I would go to Tina's house after school. I could look at her costume and tell her how great she was going to be. Maybe I could help her make some things for her act. When I told her my plans to go-go dance, I'd say I had no choice: all the mothers had wanted me in Ruby. I wouldn't even mention the cage.

Tina sat down at our old table and pointed at me. George and Karl looked over.

"Look," Betsy said, and handed me a rhinestone clip.

"We've all got one." They turned their heads so I could see the clips in their ponytails.

I wondered if Betsy was returning the one Artie had stolen from me, or if that one was in Mona's ponytail.

But I didn't want to make a fuss. I'd just accept it and then throw it in the garbage.

"Put it on," Betsy said, and stood up behind me, running her fingers through my hair to pull it into a ponytail. I put the clip around it.

"Yay!" They clapped.

"Wait till you see your costume," Mona said.

⁂

I passed Tina a note in class, telling her I'd come to her house after school. It was my mother's late day, so as long as I made it home before her, I didn't have to ask permission.

On the way there, Tina kept yakking and not giving me a chance to get a word in edgewise. I think she knew I was going to tell her something she didn't want to hear. She talked about visiting Amherst one day and surprising Kirby. And how her mother wanted to take a trip. And the cool stuff she was making for her act.

Mostly I wasn't listening. I was rehearsing in my mind what I'd tell her as soon as we got to her house.

But when we got there, the door was locked and Tina didn't have a key. She didn't say anything and ran around to try the back door.

It was locked too. Tina sat on the back stoop and looked at her feet.

"What are you going to do?" I asked her.

"My mother will be home any minute," she said. "Maybe you shouldn't stay, though."

"You want me to wait in case your mother doesn't come back?" I asked.

"No. It's all right. Really. I can ride you home on my bike if you want."

It was two miles, but I preferred to walk. "Want to come to my house?" I asked her. Who knew when her mother was really coming back. Tina could be stuck out in the cold for hours.

"Thanks. I'll just wait." Tina stuck her hands in her jacket pockets and crossed her legs. "You go ahead."

I was relieved not to have to tell her about Ruby. But as I turned to leave, I was filled with such dread of spending another night worrying about breaking the news to her, I just blurted it out. "Tina, Betsy asked me to join her band. I'm going to be the go-go dancer."

Tina's eyes bugged out. "Go-go dancer? Like with white boots?"

I nodded.

For a second, Tina's face fell. Then it was like a light-bulb went off over her head and she popped to her feet, excited. "Oh, my God. I have white boots. They're actually rubber but you could never tell. I could go-go dance with you!"

"Tina," I said. "You're not invited."

She blinked her eyes fast. "Can't you be in two acts? Can't you disco with me and go-go with them?"

"I really can't."

Her eyes shifted from my eyes to the ground. "Will you be my assistant in the magic act?"

"I'm sorry, Tina," I said. "But I've dreamed of being in the talent show with Betsy since kindergarten. It's like if Kirby showed up and she asked you to do something with her. You know?"

She shrugged one shoulder and still didn't look at me.

"I'd do something with you both," she said almost in a whisper.

Just then Lulu ran over. "Let's disco!" she said.

I told them I had to go.

Tina wouldn't give up. "George is going to play sound effects," she called after me. "Maybe you could stand beside him offstage and when I saw my doll in half, you could go like, 'Oooh, ouch, it hurts!' "

I shook my head. "Sorry," I said again, and started walking.

✳

Tina didn't come to school the next day and it didn't even occur to me to worry. I guess I was too relieved.

Now I could just go ahead and be the chillest, greatest go-go dancer in a cage the world had ever seen.

I wished I could practice in the cage immediately, but Betsy had told me that I wouldn't get to dance in it until the dress rehearsal the night before the show. It needed to be repaired and painted because it had rust on it.

The dress rehearsal was the Thursday coming up,

and we were going to spend Saturday afternoon of the weekend before rehearsing at Charlie's. Our plan was to finish around dinnertime and then all stay overnight for a pajama pool party.

Saturday afternoon, it was starting to get dark and we'd already run through the act about a hundred times. Finally, I felt like if I had to do the Mashed Potato one more time I'd turn into one. So while Charlie did her riff on the drums, I just let it rip. I heebie-jeebied around the room and bounced on Charlie's bed.

The band stopped in the middle. "What are you doing?" Betsy said.

"Just goofing around. Don't worry, I won't do it in the show."

"You'd better not." Mona looked at Charlie, who looked at Grace, who looked at Betsy, all with this expression on their faces like "Cuckoo."

"Ummm," Mona said. "This is a *rehearsal*?" She talked really slowly, like she needed to spell it out. "We rehearse at a rehearsal, exactly the way it's going to be in the show. It's the *purpose*?"

"All right, all *R-I-G-H-T*," I spelled.

I went back to my standard moves and tried to make it interesting by alternately dancing really fast and really slow.

After tacos followed by ice cream with crumbled-up Oreos on top, we changed into our bathing suits, ran squealing down the hall to the pool, and jumped in.

Charlie's parents never said a thing about the noise. They were probably in their own wing.

Charlie's older sister, Isabelle, came in and sat on a poolside lounge chair eating a bag of peanut M&Ms. She went to the private high school in the next town over, where Charlie would probably go too. "One more weeeeek," she said, like "Oooooh ooooooh."

"You know what I heard last night?" she went on. "The high school student who's going to make the video is one of the talent show judges. It's a boy. I don't know his name. Oh, and he graduated from Heady Hollow Elementary School." She held up her hands like we were going to assault her with a million questions. "That's all I know."

The third judge was Ms. Janet, my old ballet teacher.

"I hope he's cute," Mona said.

"Like he's going to be all over a bunch of fifth graders? Try not to let your heads get *too* big," Isabelle said as she got up to leave. "Oh, and don't keep me up all night or I'll throw your instruments in the pool."

✳

After dinner on Sunday, Betsy came over to hang out for the first time in what seemed like a year. My mother was so happy she was visiting, she gave us each an extra-big piece of pumpkin pie with whipped cream and let us eat it in my room.

In preparation for having Betsy over, I'd picked up all my clothes and lit a scented candle: cinnamon. Betsy sat at one end of the bed and I sat at the other. "The old room," she said, looking around.

"The old room," I repeated.

"You still play with her?" she pointed her fork at Katie.

"Not really. No."

"My dolls are up in the attic. My mother's going to give them to my cousin Amanda."

"All my cousins are older than me," I said, as though it would explain why Katie still sat on my bureau, which it didn't really.

"The other day when you and Mona and I were walking down the street," I said, "did you think we were like Charlie's Angels?"

"Our hair's the wrong colors."

I wasn't talking about it like that. Like we were *exact* duplicates. But it wasn't worth explaining.

"You know," I said. "I had the idea to be your go-go dancer a long time ago, before I taught Tina to disco."

"Really?"

I didn't want to tell Betsy that the reason I never approached her was because she'd laughed so hard on the bus at that embarrassing poem I'd written about losing her.

And Betsy didn't ask why I'd never told her my go-go idea, probably because she didn't want to bring up how mean she'd been to me.

"Tina's so funny-looking," Betsy said. "And weird."

"I know," I said. "Doesn't she look like she could have a pet snake?"

"Gerbils," Betsy said. "An ant farm. Bats."

To make it even, I switched to making fun of Mona. "How much time do you think Mona spends drying her hair every morning?"

"I don't know." I guess Betsy didn't want to play the game about *her* friend. "I asked for my own blow-dryer for my birthday," she said.

I thought of telling her about how my cousin Francesca had visited, and about how much our breasts are going to itch when they grow. But I was too afraid Betsy already knew that breasts itched and would think I was immature for believing I was telling her something new.

"How'd you get to know Ms. Creeley?" Betsy asked, and I told her the whole thing about the poems Ms. Creeley had asked Tina and me to write.

"What's it like answering her phones?" I wanted to know.

"It's cool," she said, and then made her voice all

formal and said, " 'Ms. Creeley's office, may I help you?' And I get to see who gets sent to the office. Like once Jack Ramey came in all crying because he got caught cheating."

Remembering my own crying, I changed the subject to a happier one. "When we get our video, we can send it to *American Idol.* They're probably going to have a junior show. They'll send a talent scout here to watch us in person."

"Do they really do that, or is this another one of your fantasies?"

Half the time I forgot that they *were* fantasies. "That's *probably* how they do it," I said.

Betsy took a deep breath, sounding annoyed.

"Okay," I said, and sat up tall. "What do *you* want to talk about?"

"My mother said I could only stay for half an hour." She stood and picked up her dish.

* Chapter Twenty-three *

On the bus, I walked past George in the front seat to sit with Betsy and Mona. It felt strange to have Mona's leg pressing against mine and to see George up front all alone, his violin case peeking above his shoulder. I wished I'd at least said hello to him, and didn't know why I hadn't. I guessed it was because he was on the Tina team and I wasn't. And since I'd stopped sitting with him and Karl at lunch, I was afraid he wouldn't say hello back.

In class, I discovered Tina was absent again. This time I was worried. The doors to her house had been locked the last time I'd seen her, almost a week before. I'd called once over the weekend and no one had answered. And here we were at the beginning of talent show week and she was nowhere. Her mother could have forgotten she even had a daughter, like she'd forgotten her daughter's stuffed monkey.

I decided to stop by Ms. Creeley's on my way to the bus after school to ask her if she knew anything.

As I carried my tray over to Ruby's table at lunch, I imagined that the whole cafeteria was watching me, and instead of everyone being relieved they weren't me, they were wishing they *were* me. Every time I laughed, or when Charlie gave me her Jell-O, I saw it all from the outside, as though I were still sitting with George and Karl and Tina, on the outside looking in.

Then after lunch Karl bumped shoulders with me in the hall. "Hey," he said.

"Hey," I said.

"You hear from Tina?" he asked me.

"I called this weekend but nobody answered."

"You think she took a trip or something?"

"You think?" I hadn't thought of that.

"Could be. But I have no idea, really. You're in their band?" he asked, meaning Ruby.

"Isn't it cool?" I tried to sound perky.

"Cool," he said, "depends on your perspective."

At the end of the day, Ms. Creeley was running out of her office as I was running in. When I asked if Tina's mother had called to say Tina was sick. But Ms. Creeley just said, "Oh, Ally, hi," and rushed past.

I thought of returning to Ms. Creeley's the next day, but at the last moment, I didn't do it.

Betsy, Mona, Charlie, Gracie, and I practiced every afternoon that week. Charlie's sister, who had watched the band before I'd joined, came a few times and said Ruby was better than ever.

Everyone in the band except for me and Mona were going to wear stretchy ruby-sequined pants with their belly buttons showing and black tube tops with "Ruby" written across them in ruby sequins. Also black chokers around their necks, ruby red lipstick, and sky blue sparkly eye shadow. Plus fake microphones like Madonna's on their ears. Charlie's sister had made them.

Mona and I would wear stretchy ruby-sequined miniskirts, black tights, and the same black tube tops with Ruby written across. Mona would hold a real microphone, and I'd wear her white go-go boots.

Thursday, the night before dress rehearsal, Mona's mother brought us to the community theater where the cage had been stored. A truck was going to pick it up the next day and bring it to school. Meanwhile, it had been pulled to the middle of the stage for me to test it out. It was as big as those spinning cages they have on some Ferris wheels.

When I saw it I broke out in goose bumps.

"There once was a girl in a gilded cage, ding dong, ding dong." Mona's mother, Paige, sang some weird old-time song. "This used to have a swing in it," she said as she opened the door. "But we removed it for you."

"Cool." I walked slowly around it, running my hands over the wire mesh.

"Go ahead, Ally, step in," Paige said. She looked just

like Mona, only her hair was reddish gold instead of blond. She wore lime green shoes with heels and no backs and lime green pants that were baggy in the legs but tight around the hips. She was so thin and pretty she could have been a model.

I stepped into the cage as Mona's mother slipped a CD into a boom box, of Aretha Franklin singing "Respect."

It was one thing to dance while the band played, but it was another to dance with all of them standing there watching, including Mona's mother. "You want me to dance?" I asked.

"You have to," said Betsy.

"Tomorrow's dress rehearsal," said Mona.

"It feels strange," I said.

"Once you start you'll feel fine," said Paige. Then she did a really sad interpretation of the Pony.

Slowly at first, then in time to the music, I did the Jerk and then the Mashed Potato. There wasn't too much room in the cage.

When the song finished, Paige clapped. "You are a natural, Ally. What a gift. Truly."

"We told you," Mona said to her mother.

By dress rehearsal, the cage had been delivered to school. Four chains at its corners were attached to a central chain that cranked up to the rafters. The cage would remain hidden throughout the talent show. Ruby would go on last, after Harry Crick, the stilt walker.

At dress rehearsal everything is supposed to go exactly like it would in the real show, so we had to sit in Ms. Wiley's room and wait while everyone else performed. "Listen carefully," Ms. Wiley said before we began. "As soon as the act in front of you goes onstage, you will proceed to the wings, and then take the stage immediately after. When you leave the stage, go directly to Ms. Summers's next door, and wait. Only those of you who haven't yet performed belong in this room. Is that clear?"

Everyone nodded.

"As soon as the last act, Ruby, returns to the room, all of you line up in the order you performed and then I'll lead you to the stage. Onstage, form a horseshoe and take a well-deserved bow. On Saturday it will be a little different. You'll wait ten minutes before I lead you out. We need to give the judges time to make their decision. Then, when the winners are announced, applaud and try to be genuinely happy for your friends."

The lower grades, including kindergarten, had been invited to the dress rehearsal to give us the feeling of an audience, and, of course, to let them see us.

I felt bad that Tina wasn't even going to get to do magic. She might have been looking forward to the talent show more than anybody in the whole school.

While we waited, Betsy, Mona, Charlie, and Gracie went over and over the lines of the song. They said it was a technique actors use that they'd learned from Mona's mother.

My hands were sweating and I was breathing too fast.

As soon as Harry Crick went on, we moved to the wings. To calm myself, I breathed deeply and reminded myself how impressed Mona's mother had been and how I'd danced alone in front of everyone and done just fine.

We watched as Harry, dressed like Abe Lincoln, juggled hoops and then oranges while standing on stilts that made him twice as tall as me. The second he walked off-stage, the curtain closed, and we stepped on. Mr. Jeweler, the janitor, cranked down the cage, and I stepped into it as the other girls picked up their instruments. Then, as I held on to the sides, Mr. Jeweler cranked me up.

The cage felt strange and wobbly. Far below, I could see the heads of Ruby. I started to sweat. I was afraid I'd fall.

The curtain began to rise. I could hardly breathe. When it was high enough for the kids in the audience to see the cage and me in it, I heard gasps, and then cheers. I couldn't make out faces, just silhouettes of heads above seats, and the blindingly bright lights high up in the back of the auditorium that lit the stage.

Now Charlie began to count, "A one and a two and a three." Ruby played their first notes and I began to Mashed Potato. As long as I did standing-in-place dances in the middle of the cage, it hardly moved and I could keep my balance. I did the Jerk, the Pony, the Swim. When I Hitchhiked the top of my body to one side, the cage swung a little. I did it to the other side and it swung in the opposite direction. I Hitchhiked with my whole body and the cage swung for real. I did it until the cage swung from one side of the stage to the other. The audience cheered. And my whole body smiled.

When the song ended, Ms. Wiley jumped to her feet clapping, and so did the audience. The cage was lowered. I stepped out and all of Ruby surrounded me for a hug.

It was over too quickly. I wished it were Saturday night already, right *now*. I couldn't wait to dance again, and was already thinking of ways to do it better.

Walking off the stage with Ruby, hanging on to them, jumping up and down, I knew my days of being Ally the Weirdo Crybaby were over. Kids in kindergarten had watched me and now probably couldn't wait to be the stars of the fifth-grade talent show too. They probably wanted to be just like me.

Ms. Creeley had been so right. Being onstage, especially when you get a standing ovation, changes your life.

✳ Chapter Twenty-four ✳

On show night all the performers in the Heady Hollow Annual Fifth-Grade Talent Show gathered in Ms. Wiley's room.

The Adams twins practiced tossing their hats in the air and catching them. Mitsy Patrick twirled her baton. Stu and Artie had on their Tae Kwon Do outfits that looked like pajamas. Stu traded football cards with the two wrestlers in a corner while Artie sat in another corner by himself.

At six on the dot, Ms. Wiley reminded us of the rules and asked if there were any questions.

"Can we go get brownies at intermission?" Stu asked.

The PTA was selling home-baked pastries for a dollar apiece.

"I guess I can't keep you cooped up in here all night.

But get your refreshments and come right back. Are there any more questions?"

"Is it true that one of the judges is the same kid who's going to make the video of the winners?" Charlie asked.

"A very talented young man who won a national award with one of his videos. He graduated from Heady Hollow and is now a sophomore at East Meadow High."

Artie raised his hand. "What if you change your mind and don't want to do it anymore?"

"Do what? The show?" Ms. Wiley asked.

Artie looked scared.

"Arthur, I am not going to force anyone to do anything. But I have a feeling that if you do drop out, you'll regret it. Ten seconds after you step onto that stage, magic happens. Everything slows down, because you are feeling the energy of all those people focused on you. Don't worry, Arthur. I just bet you'll be a little more careful this time and you won't fall. People will be flabbergasted when they see how high you can kick. Am I right, Stuart?"

Stu grunted yes.

"All right then. We have nearly twenty minutes before showtime. People have begun to arrive, so keep the volume down."

At that moment, the door opened, and who should walk in carrying two shopping bags but . . . Tina! Her ponytail was pulled through the back of her baseball cap, and her pink leggings looked even shorter than the first time she'd worn them.

"Tina!" I shouted before I knew what I was doing.

"Tina. We'd given up on you," Ms. Wiley said.

"My grandfather always says, 'Never give up.' And I always say, 'What about the *Titanic?*'"

"Does Ms. Creeley know you're here?" Ms. Wiley asked.

"Yes. She was supposed to tell you."

"I'm sure it just slipped her mind. She's got a million things to think about. All right, I'll tell you what. You'll go last. I think we can manage that."

"But *we're* last," Betsy said.

"You *were* last. Now you're second to last."

"But the cage," Betsy said.

"Ally will climb out, then we'll crank it back up. No big deal."

Betsy narrowed her eyes at Tina.

"You're going to be in a cage?" Tina ran up to me. "I *love* your outfit."

"Where . . . were . . . you?" I lowered my voice to ask her.

"It's complicated. I'll tell you later. It's kind of mysterious. Anyway, I'm doing magic. Look." She pulled a Care Bear out of her shopping bag and dangled it in front of my face, then dropped it back in the bag. "If you dance with me, we could get George to play his violin. It's not too late."

"Tina! I *can't*."

I couldn't believe it was the night of the show and she still wouldn't give up. And she wouldn't answer my question about where she'd been. "Tina . . . where were you? And why is everything always 'complicated' and 'mysterious'?"

She didn't answer me. She just started pulling stuff out of her shopping bag. Besides the Care Bear there was a cardboard hat, a silk coat, and a newspaper. Her hands seemed kind of shaky. If Tina were a person who could cry, it seemed like she would have been crying now.

"Look!" she shouted, and dropped the Care Bear in the top hat to demonstrate her trick. Now the whole room was looking. "I'll say I'm going to pull a rabbit out of the hat. Only instead of a rabbit it'll be—" She pulled the Care Bear out. "A RAT!" She dangled it in front of my face and it hit me in the nose.

I swatted at it.

"From far away it'll look just like a rat, especially when I scream, 'A rat!'" Which she screamed right then.

Ms. Wiley ran back into the room. "Tina, please! Keep it down."

The whole room snickered. Tina put her hand over her mouth and made her eyes go wide, but it seemed fake. Then she whispered, "If Lulu comes, she'll run screaming out of the auditorium. Then the whole audience will scream and run too!"

That was ridiculous; the whole audience would never run out.

Even though part of me wanted nothing more than to get away from her, I put my hand on her arm and said, "Tina."

"Ally, come here. I have something to tell you," Betsy called.

I walked over and Tina followed.

"Can we please talk in *private*?" Betsy asked fake politely, looking straight at Tina. The band had arranged their chairs in a circle. There was an empty chair for me.

Tina cut her eyes over to me like she expected me to stick up for her.

I looked down at my feet, took my seat, and didn't look up until I saw Tina's feet walk away.

"You're supposed to be with *us*," Betsy said.

"I am with you."

I looked at the other girls and they were all staring at me.

When I finally looked over at Tina, she had her silk coat on and was tying scarves together.

✳

Ms. Creeley came in a few minutes before six-thirty. She'd combed her hair back off her face and fixed it with styling gel. She wore diamond earrings and heels that probably made her taller than every man in the audience. Her pink lipstick was shiny, and her deep blue dress matched her eyes. The dress had a V-neck and flared a little at the knees. She was beautiful.

"Look at all of you." She glowed. "Like real performers. Tina," she said, then walked over and held Tina's hand. "You've all worked very hard for this night. Now it's time to stop working and have fun. I know I'm going to enjoy sitting in the audience watching you.

"I realize there's been a lot of excitement about the possibility of being on TV and winning five hundred dollars. This is the first year that the talent show has been a competition, and there were very good reasons why we never did this before. We wanted to build confidence and to foster a spirit of joy in performing for the sake of performing—and providing entertainment. Performing is an act of generosity. You give others enjoyment. I'd like you all to think of that while you're out there on that stage tonight."

Then, "Artie?" Ms. Creeley said. "Is something the matter?"

I turned and saw Artie Kaminsky with his face in his hands. He shook his head no but didn't look like he meant it.

"Come on outside." She put her hand on his shoulder and steered him out the door.

I know it's mean to be glad that someone else is upset. But Artie Kaminsky's crying before the talent show was a dream come true. I raised my hand and asked for permission to go to the restroom. I wanted to see this up close.

I walked into the hall, but Artie and Ms. Creeley had already disappeared. I decided to go to the restroom anyway. On my way I saw George and Karl by the door to the lighting booth. George was carrying his violin.

Seeing them standing there, I felt a little tug on my heart and realized I'd missed them. "You're playing sound effects for Tina?" I asked. "How'd you know she was back?"

"She called me this morning."

"Do you know where Tina *was*?" I asked him.

George shook his head.

"When did you guys practice?"

"We didn't. All I have to do is make sound effects." George shrugged.

"I'm going to put a purple gel over the spotlight to make it weird and eerie," Karl said. "Mr. Martinez, the lighting man, doesn't care."

"Do you know when Tina's on?" George asked.

"Last. So if you're in the show, why aren't you backstage?" I asked George.

"Because nobody knows I'm in it but you and Tina and Karl."

I really looked at them then. George had on his regulation khaki pants, red jersey, black shoes, and white socks, and Karl's hair was so messy he might not have combed it since his last haircut. They were nerdy but they were interesting and nice—and they were talented in a good way. George didn't use his talent to make him popular. He probably didn't even *want* to be popular.

But most importantly, George and Karl were loyal friends. And I wasn't.

✳ Chapter Twenty-five ✱

By intermission half the kids had finished their acts and vanished into Ms. Summers's room. The fewer kids there were left in Ms. Wiley's room, the meaner I felt not talking to Tina.

As Ruby whisper-sang "Respect" for about the one hundredth time, I glanced around to see what Tina was doing. She'd changed into black tights and a white shirt and was coloring the rim of her top hat black with a marker.

When Ruby finally stopped whisper-singing, Mona said, "Let's all tell our wishes. Not the one on your last birthday cake or your next birthday cake. Because then they won't come true. But if you had two wishes, what would your second one be?"

Everyone said winning the talent show. I wondered

what their first wishes would be, because if it were my birthday today I'd wish for winning the talent show. I said I'd wish for a sister my own age.

"That's a twin," Betsy said.

"But it's a wish, so it can be impossible. I'd be the oldest by like three months."

"That's dumb," Betsy said.

"Totally," Mona agreed.

"Especially if you want the wish to come true," Charlie added.

"She could be adopted," Gracie suggested.

If I'd said the same thing to Tina, she'd be imagining what my sister looked like and what kind of personality she'd have. We'd be making up a whole story about my sister's and my life together.

Now the Rubies were talking about some movie they all wanted to see. I stopped listening—I wasn't that interested, and anyway, I was busy thinking about other things.

If Tina had been in the band go-go dancing with me, and she'd been rehearsing at Charlie's the other day when I'd heebie-jeebied, she'd have run right over and heebie-jeebied with me. I remembered the first time we'd danced, with Lulu. I'd done a silly tap dance and Tina had joined in without even blinking an eye. I loved that she'd asked Ms. Creeley for a Hershey's Kiss and taken a handful. My mother had been mad at her for asking for more butter for her popcorn, but Tina had wanted more butter, so she'd asked. She never changed the way she was just so people would like her.

I looked at Tina in the corner, covering the bulb on the end of her baton with tinfoil, and then I looked at Betsy huddled with Ruby in a closed circle. I had a question to ask Betsy, but it was hard to make the words come out of my mouth—maybe because I already knew the answer and I was ashamed to hear it.

I closed my eyes, breathed, then let it out. "Betsy, would you be my friend if you didn't need a go-go dancer?"

All of Ruby looked at me.

"What are you talking about?" Betsy glanced at the rest of the girls, who wouldn't look back at her.

I turned to Tina. She was listening to every word.

It was as obvious as it had always been, though I hadn't wanted to see it before. The Rubies were not my friends.

I waited another moment, and then I stood up and stepped out of their circle. "I quit," I said calmly.

"Are you *crazy*?" Betsy stood too. "You can't *quit*."

"My best friend needs a magic assistant," I said. "Sorry." I walked over to Tina.

Tina did that arm-circle-going-in-the-opposite-direction-of-the-hip-circle thing.

"Why are you being like this?" Betsy called a little too loudly.

"And what about the cage?" Mona stood. "My mother went to a lot of trouble to borrow it. She hired the truck to bring it here at her own expense."

"I'm sorry," I said. "I should've never joined you. Please tell your mother I feel bad about the cage."

Tina jumped up and down, then hugged me, and we jumped together. "One for all and all for one!" she cried. Then, bouncing on her toes like a jackhammer, she sang, "Thank you, Lucky Stars, and the moon, and—"

"Tina," I interrupted, resting my hands on her shoulders, calming her down. When she was still, I looked into her eyes and said, "I'm sorry I was such a bad friend. I'm so, so sorry."

Tina looked at me hard.

"It's just that I hated being laughed at," I went on.

"That's okay," Tina said at last. "I like to make people laugh. And that's okay too. Right?"

"Right."

✳ Chapter Twenty-six ✳

When Ruby went to perform, Tina put on her wizard hat and black cape. I kept on my Ruby outfit but turned the tube top with Ruby written across it inside out.

I helped Tina carry one of her bags to the wings. Of course, we'd had no time to rehearse even once. The plan was that she would whisper to me what I was to hand to her and then I'd just hand her things.

We watched Ruby, and it was like a light switched on in every one of them. Maybe it was the magic Ms. Wiley said happens in front of an audience, or maybe it was the extra challenge of performing without their dancer. But whatever, they were better than ever.

Tina and I held hands and peeked at the audience. I could see my parents, and behind them, Sissy and her mother. Across the aisle was Lulu, with a man who must have been her father. I hadn't told my parents about the cage because I wanted it to be a surprise. Now they were probably surprised I wasn't even dancing.

At first I couldn't find the judges, but then I saw them, sitting in the third row in the middle. Ms. Janet sat between Mrs. No Joy and the high school boy. The boy was short and had longish wavy brown hair. He was wearing a red T-shirt with a dog's head on it, and thick black glasses. He moved his head to the music, smiling.

"Are you scared?" I asked Tina. She looked totally silly in her pointed wizard's hat.

"No," she whispered. "Are you?"

"Petrified."

"Don't worry, all you have to do is act glamorous. Magicians' assistants are always glamorous. . . ." She hesitated. "You know when you and the band were making those wishes? Mine would have been to dance disco with you."

Then Ruby was squeezing past us on their way to Ms. Summers's room.

The kids working as stagehands cleared the microphones and the drums.

"Break a leg," Tina said.

"Break a leg," I said back.

We walked to the middle of the stage. I directed my gaze toward the lights in the back so I wouldn't look at the faces in the first few rows. Tina's act was supposed to be funny. But there are two kinds of laughing—the having-fun kind and the making-fun kind. I was afraid the audience would laugh the making-fun kind.

"Hello, everyone," Tina said. "Welcome to the wonderful world of magic and illusion. I'm Merlinda." She bowed. "And this is my assistant, the beautiful Natasha."

I bowed.

"I've come from Transylvania to dazzle your senses with a few of my world-famous tricks."

People shifted in their seats. It was almost ten o'clock. They were probably tired and wanted to go home. Some kids in the front row started talking, and a teacher came and shushed them.

George appeared on the opposite side of the stage, behind the curtain.

"Now for my first trick," Merlinda said. We were

214

standing inside a purple light that made a circle on the floor.

George made his violin go all shivery.

"The hat!" she said under her breath. I was supposed to hold the hat so she could pull the rabbit/Care Bear/rat out. But I didn't know that. Instead, I tried to hand it to her, and when it fell on the floor the rat dropped out.

I heard a groan.

Tina put the rat back in and handed me the hat so we could do it over. "Hold it," she whispered. I held it out to her as she waved her baton-wand, then pulled out the Care Bear and yelled, "A rat!" George's violin hit a long high note, and nobody laughed.

I handed Tina the newspaper and scissors. As she pretended to cut the newspaper into a shape, I stepped out of the purple light, and George's violin played a happy tune, like in cartoons when flowers bloom. I could hear people in the audience whispering. I couldn't help myself. I took a peek at the judges in the third row. I think Ms. Janet was sleeping, the high school boy was looking at someone in the audience instead of at the stage, and

Mrs. No Joy was staring so hard her eye beams could have drilled holes through us.

When the pieces of paper fell to the floor, Artie Kaminsky, who was sitting in the front row not crying, said, "Booooo!"

My heart hurt for Tina.

But instead of letting Artie get to her, you know what Tina did?

She kicked the pieces of paper like they were autumn leaves.

And then she skipped and kicked them again.

Someone had booed, and instead of feeling like hiding, she'd kicked and skipped.

How amazing was that?

I looked at George at the same time he looked at me.

He played a line from "Somewhere over the Rainbow"—with a disco beat.

My heart started to race. What the heck. There was only one Fifth-Grade Talent Show, and my best friend really, really wanted to dance in it.

And so did I.

I couldn't believe I did it, even as I did it. I disco-walked to Tina, placed my hand in the middle of her back, and spun her out. Karl jiggled the spotlight and I reeled her back in. We looked in each other's eyes, threw our heads back, lifted a leg high, and Tango-Hustled across the stage. Then I spun Tina so she whirled like a top. We did a Hustle-Hitchhike. Then George changed the song to "Moondance," in a weirdly wild, crazy jazz beat. Karl made the spotlight revolve around and around the stage. Somebody in the audience yelped, "Yeah!" Tina and I looked at each other, and all of a sudden the last thing I wanted to be was stiff. The magic had happened on the stage, and I wanted to be free and wild and full of jumping beans. I wanted to be *me*.

And so I went for it. I heebie-jeebied all over the stage, and Tina joined right in. We bumped into each other and heebie-jeebied some more.

People in the audience were on their feet.

The next time we came together, Tina whispered, "The jump!" I started to say "NO!" but it was too late. We walked with attitude backward for four steps and stopped. I bent my knees, planted my feet wide apart, and imagined I was the giant old oak in my yard as Tina came flying toward me, jumped, and wrapped her legs around my waist. I spun her as she bent backward, the tips of her fingers grazing the ground. I spun and spun her until George signaled with the music that it was time for a change. I let her down. She put her hand on my shoulder and we disco-walked offstage.

The audience clapped and hollered and whistled, still on their feet. One person yelled, "Encore!"

We ran back out and bowed.

Finally we left the stage.

In the wings, Ms. Wiley hugged us. "Unbelievable," she said, before walking out to tell the audience that we would have a ten-minute break to allow the judges to make their decision.

✳ Chapter Twenty-seven ✳

As we entered Ms. Summers's room, Tina said, "That was more fun than waltzing in the *Hindenburg*."

"And I thought it was going to be as bad as catching fire in the *Hindenburg*," I said.

"Shhhh!" Betsy held her finger to her lips. "We're supposed to be quiet."

At last it was time to file back onto the stage in the order we'd performed. Ms. Creeley stood in the middle of the horseshoe space we'd formed, holding a piece of paper.

"Thank you, everyone. It's been a long and entertaining night. Our kids have worked very hard. They're all winners, but unfortunately there's only one prize." She turned her back to the audience to face us. "I just want you to know how incredible you are. It takes guts to do what you did tonight, and a sense of humor. You were all champs, and we are proud of you." She winked at me and Tina.

She turned back to the audience. "And now, the moment we've all been waiting for. The winner of the Annual Heady Hollow Fifth-Grade Talent Show is . . ." She unfolded the paper. *"Ruby!"*

Betsy, Mona, Charlie, and Gracie ran to Ms. Creeley, laughing and jumping up and down.

The other kids in the horseshoe and I clapped politely as we'd been instructed. I was disappointed—Tina and I had gotten a standing ovation and they hadn't.

Tina said, "Booooo," in my ear.

And I booooooed back in hers.

✱

"You would have been a winner," Tina said as we walked offstage and headed toward Ms. Summers's room.

"Oh, well," I said. "But we did have the Time of Our

Lives." "The Time of My Life" was the last dance song in *Dirty Dancing.*

Mrs. No Joy was in the middle of Ms. Summers's room, putting on her coat. "Hi, Mrs. Joy." Tina beamed. "How'd you like our dance?"

Tina's beaming always irritated Mrs. No Joy. "Dance? Is that what you call that ridiculous display?"

"Mrs. Joy." Ms. Creeley interrupted. She had come in with the high school boy who was going to make the video. "You and I are going to have a few words. I'll thank you to leave this room. Now."

"I will not be treated like a child," Mrs. No Joy said, then stomped off and slammed the door.

"Don't listen to a word she said," Ms. Creeley told us, looking from Tina to me. "You were mesmerizing. Amazing. Believe it."

Tina and I smiled.

"I voted for you," the high school boy said, and bowed with one hand in front of his waist and one in back. Up close I recognized him. He was the kid on my favorite show on cable, *The Devil Take It.* "That was some crazy dancing you did," he said. "Really glad to meet you." He held out one hand to Tina and one to me. When we gave him ours, he didn't shake, but slid his hands toward himself, then hopped and blew on his fingers like they'd been burnt. "Hot!" he said. "What're your names?"

Tina and I introduced ourselves.

"Hey, my name's Miller too. Freddy."

"YOU'RE FREDDY MILLER!"

"You've heard of me?"

"Everybody thinks I'm your sister. I thought you were a juvenile delinquent."

Ms. Creeley laughed. "Let's say Freddy's an original."

"Square peg, round hole." Freddy jabbed his thumb to his chest. "Like you guys. Maybe we are related. Keep dancing. That violin player, who is he?"

We'd lost George.

"He's a prodigy," I said.

"I'm going to get him to do the sound track for my video. It's about the night John Lennon died."

222

George was standing at the door, and Freddy skipped once, then walked quickly over to him.

Tina and I looked at each other and burst out laughing.

You don't only laugh when things are funny. Sometimes you laugh when you're just plain happy.

Chapter Twenty-eight

The next day Tina called and asked if I could come to her house.

I rode my bike over after lunch. She was sitting on her top step in her mother's silk coat, waiting. "Pull," she said, holding out her arm.

I grabbed the tip of a scarf peeking out from her sleeve and pulled and pulled until a pile of brightly patterned, tied-together scarves made a mound at my feet.

"Cool. Your mom home?" I asked.

She shook her head.

I'd had a feeling she wouldn't be. "I'm not supposed to come to your house unless your mother's here," I finally told Tina. "My father's rule. I never told you before. Let's go to my house."

"It's okay," Tina said. "My grandfather's here."

"He is?" It was strange she hadn't introduced me to him first thing. "Inside?" I asked, looking in the window to see if I could spot him.

"He's giving us a chance to talk. He told me I had to tell you."

"Tell me what? Is your mother sick?" I asked.

Tina nodded, and I sat next to her. "What happened?"

Tina rubbed her knee with the heel of her hand like it itched. "Oh, it's just that . . . I mean, you noticed how strange she acts sometimes."

"Yes."

"That's part of her illness."

"Bipolar." I remembered.

"She's not always like that. When she takes her medication, she's normal. It's just that almost as soon as we moved here, she stopped taking it. When she stops, she gets worse and worse, and then she has to go to the hospital."

"Is she in the hospital?"

Tina shook her head, looking at the ground.

"Where is she? What's happened? Tina, tell me."

"She went to Las Vegas. She said she was going to marry Sam Carpacci. Remember she talked about him? He doesn't even exist. It's called a delusion. Sometimes she even thinks she's different people. She does stuff like thinks she's Madonna and calls Michael Jackson to ask him if she can borrow his plane. You know the sports car? We don't have the money for that. They already repossessed it."

"Where is she now?"

"I don't know. She's missing."

"Are the police looking for her?"

Tina nodded.

"Are you worried?"

Tina nodded.

"Do you want to cry?"

Tina nodded.

I put my arm around her shoulder and she leaned her head into my neck, but she didn't cry. "I have to go live with my grandfather," she said.

"Oh, no!" I said.

"I'm leaving tomorrow."

"You can't. What about school?"

"I know. . . ." She sighed, then sat up and looked at me. "I'll have to go on Rock Island."

"Can't your grandfather move here until after school lets out?"

"I asked him. He says no."

"This is horrible," I said, feeling a knot form in my throat, but I stopped myself from crying. Tina already felt bad enough. She was the one whose mother was missing. She was the one who had to leave and be the new girl in the middle of a school year. "It'll be okay," I told her, putting my arm around her again to squeeze closer. "You'll be on Rock Island! You love it there. They'll find your mother."

"I hope," Tina said. "They probably will. They always have. . . ." After a moment, she said, "Ally?"

"Yeah?"

"If your parents will let you visit, my grandfather says you could stay the whole summer."

"On Rock Island?"

It would be a dream come true.

"We can go out on his sailboat, collect beach glass and make jewelry, go to that beach where the seagulls are. There's a yard sale on the Fourth of July every year at the firehouse. You pay five dollars and get to fill a whole grocery bag. Sometimes someone has died and the family contributes everything from their house. You can find the coolest antiques. I got real Mickey Mouse ears from the fifties once."

More than anything in the world I wanted to go, but it was such a long shot. "I don't know if my parents will let me," I said.

"I'll send them pictures so they can see what it's like. My grandfather can call them up. He used to be a professor. He's very responsible."

"Maybe they'll let me," I said, and decided right then that they had to. "I'll beg on my knees," I said. "I'll vacuum the whole house every week. I'll make them breakfast in bed on Sundays."

"Ally?" Tina bumped my shoulder. "In your poem,

when the Lovely Lady gave the Man in the Moon a piece of pie? Was it apple?"

"Yeah."

"With vanilla ice cream?"

I hadn't thought of that, but it seemed right. "Yes," I said.

"Want to see if we can get an apple pie and ice cream at the Seven-Eleven?"

"Sure."

"Grandpa!" Tina called. "Can I have some money?"

"Come again, Acorn?" Tina's grandfather came to the door. He was small and bald and looked a little like Yoda, which might have explained the Princess Leia hair. "Ally?" he said, looking at me.

I stood up and said, "Yes."

"I'm Joe." He stepped out the door and shook my hand. "I've heard a lot about you. I'm delighted to meet you." And then he asked Tina, "Did you have a good talk?"

"Yes. And now we're starving for pie and ice cream. Can we buy some?"

"Pie à la mode. Good idea," he said, lifting his wallet from his back pocket and giving her a twenty-dollar bill. "Pick me up the *Times* if they have one.

"I saw you and Tina in the show last night," Joe said to me. "There's only one word to describe your performance: *breathtaking*."

"That's two words," Tina said.

"No, it is not." He rubbed the top of her head. "Now go get your pie."

We walked across the empty parking lot until Tina stopped by the big oak and looked at me. "You did what you were most scared to do," she said. "You danced with me."

I laughed. It was true.

"Let's wish on our Lucky Stars every night until you come to Rock Island," she said.

"Every night." I licked my fingers and crossed my heart.

"Hey," Tina said. "Let's make up our own sign."

I didn't even have to think. I raised my arms and bumped her hip.

Tina did the same move back.

"The Bump," I said, and then we did the Bump, giggling until my belly hurt and I felt like crying all over again. My eyes filled with tears.

"It's all right," Tina said. "You can cry. I would if I could."

And that's when I noticed Tina's pop-out ears. They weren't funny at all anymore—they were beautiful, like butterfly wings.

I decided crying could wait till I got home. "I'm too starved for pie," I said.

"You and me and the Man in the Moon," Tina said, aiming a cheerleader's jump up at the sky, and then we ran the rest of the way.

ear Tina,

You will die. Freddy Miller invited me to be in the video he's making about the night John Lennon died! It takes place in the eighties and I have to learn a new dance called the Pogo. Basically you jump like you're on a pogo stick only with your arms glued to your sides. I have to pogo at a punk club and wear makeup. George is composing original music, and Karl has to walk around with a big fuzzy microphone on a pole. He's the sound man.

Betsy and Mona promised to show me the video Freddy made of Ruby as soon as they get it back from the state competition. They're supposed to hear if they're finalists on February 15. They aren't so bad as long as I'm not trying to be their best friend. I sit with

George on the bus every day, and they sit right behind us. I think they're all impressed because Freddy Miller likes us.

Here's the best. One day at the bus stop, Artie threw a black rubber spider at me, and Mona said, "I think Artie's in love with you." Then she sang, "Artie loves Ally." Betsy joined in, and then everybody did. Now, Thank you, Lucky Stars, Artie avoids me like I'm covered with boils.

I'm going with George and his mother to hear George in a concert in New York City! George says that in the spring he might play in Providence, Rhode Island. He says it's not far from Rock Island. Do you think your grandfather would drive you there???? Please, beg him on your knees. And then maybe I could go too!

Whenever I ask my parents about Rock Island this summer, they say, "Tina can visit you too, you know." Ugh. Summer in East Meadow makes me think of a mosquito in my room. But my parents want me to sign up for swimming lessons, which is a good sign. I bet they're afraid I might drown if I visit.

I hope you're not missing your mother too much. I'm glad her hospital's nearby.

Thank you for the picture of the seagulls. I forgot that they all stand on one leg! It's like a miracle. When I visit, we should stand on one leg with them.

George and Karl say hi.

I miss you so much.

I wish on my Lucky Stars every night that I'll be seeing you real soon.

Your best friend,

Ally

P.S. I forgot to ask you, where'd you get your plaid tights?